APPLES,

RIPE AND ROSY, SIR

AND OTHER STORIES FOR BOYS AND GIRLS

MARY CATHERINE CRAWLEY

1st WORLD
LIBRARY
Literary Society

Apples, Ripe and Rosy, Sir

Mary Catherine Crowley

© 1st World Library – Literary Society, 2004
PO Box 2211
Fairfield, IA 52556
www.1stworldlibrary.org
First Edition

LCCN: 2005901357

Softcover ISBN: 1-4218-1172-3
Hardcover ISBN: 1-4218-1072-7
eBook ISBN: 1-4218-1272-X

Purchase *"Apples, Ripe and Rosy, Sir"*
as a traditional bound book at:
www.1stWorldLibrary.org/purchase.asp?ISBN=1-4218-1172-3

1st World Library Literary Society is a nonprofit organization dedicated to promoting literacy by:

- Creating a free internet library accessible from any computer worldwide.
- Hosting writing competitions and offering book publishing scholarships.

**Readers interested in supporting literacy through sponsorship, donations or membership please contact:
literacy@1stworldlibrary.org
Check us out at: www.1stworldlibrary.ORG
and start downloading free ebooks today.**

Apples, Ripe and Rosy, Sir
contributed by Tim, Ed & Rodney
in support of
1st World Library Literary Society

CONTENTS

"APPLES, RIPE AND ROSY, SIR"

I.

What a month of March it was! And after an unusually mild season, too. Old Winter seemed to have hoarded up all his stock of snow and cold weather, and left it as an inheritance to his wild and rollicking heir, that was expending it with lavish extravagance.

March was a jolly good fellow though, in spite of his bluster and boisterous ways. There was a wealth of sunshine in his honest heart, and he evidently wanted to render everybody happy. He appeared to have entered into a compact with Santa Claus to make it his business to see that the boys and girls should not, in the end, be deprived of their fair share of the season's merrymaking; that innumerable sleds and toboggans and skates, which had laid idle since Christmas, and been the objects of much sad contemplation, should have their day, after all.

And he was not really inconsiderate of the poor either; for though, very frequently, in a spirit of mischief, he and his chum Jack frost drew caricatures of spring flowers on their window-panes, knocked at their doors only to run away in a trice, and played other pranks upon them, they did not feel the same dread of all this that they would have felt in December. He would make up for it by being on his best and balmiest behavior for some days following; would promise that milder weather, when the need and the price of coal would be less, was surely coming; and that both the wild blossoms of the country fields, and the stray dandelions which struggle into bloom in city yards, would be on time, as usual.

On the special day with which we have to do, however, March was not in "a melting mood." On the contrary, the temperature was sharp and frosty, the ground white, the clouds heavy with snow. The storm of the night before had only ceased temporarily; it would begin again soon, - indeed a few flakes were already floating in the air. At four o'clock in the afternoon the children commenced to troop out of the schools. How pleasant to watch them! - to see the great doors swing open and emit, now a throng of bright-eyed, chattering little girls, in gay cloaks and hoods and mittens; or again a crowd of sturdy boys, - a few vociferating and disputing, others trudging along discussing games and sports, and others again indulging in a little random snowballing of their comrades, by the way. Half an hour later the snow was falling thick and fast. The boys were in their element. A number of them had gathered in one of the parks or squares for which the garden-like city of E --- is noted, and were busy completing a snow-fort. The jingle of sleigh-bells became less frequent, however; people hurried home; it was sure to be a disagreeable evening.

These indications were dolefully noted by one person in particular, to whom they meant more than to others in general. This was the good old Irishwoman who kept the apple and peanut stand at the street corner, and was the centre of attraction to the children on their way to and from school.

"Wisha, this is goin' to be a wild night, I'm thinkin'!" sighed she, wrapping a faded and much-worn "broshay" shawl more securely about her, and striving to protect both herself and her wares beneath the shelter of a dilapidated umbrella, one of the ribs of which had parted company with the cotton covering, - escaped from its moorings, as it were, and stood out independently. "Glory be to God, but what bad luck I've had the day!" she continued under her breath, from habit still scanning the faces of the passers-by, though she had now faint hope that any would pause to purchase. "An' it's a bigger lot than usual I laid in, too. The peanuts is extry size; an' them

MARY CATHERINE CROWLEY

Baldwins look so fine and rosy, I thought it ud make anybody's mouth water to see them. I counted upon the schoolb'ys to buy them up in a twinklin', by reason of me markin' them down to two for a cent. An' so they would, but they're so taken up with sportin' in the snow that they can think of nothin' else. An' now that it's turned so raw, sure I'm afraid it's cold comfort any one but a lad would think it, settin' his teeth on edge tryin' to eat them. I'll tarry a bit longer; an' then, if no better fortune comes, I'll take meself to me little room, even though I'll have to drink me tea without a tint of milk or a dust of sugar the night, and be thankful for that same."

Patiently she waited. The clock struck five. As no other customers appeared, the old woman, who was known as Widow Barry, concluded that she would be moving. "Though it is too bad," she murmured; "an' this the best stand anywhere hereabouts."

In reality, the stand consisted of a large basket, a camp-seat, the tiresome privilege of leaning against two feet of stone-wall, and the aforesaid umbrella, which was intended to afford, not only a roof, but an air of dignity to the concern, and was therefore always open, rain or shine.

To "shut up shop," though it meant simply to lower the umbrella, gather up the goods and depart, was to the apple-vender a momentous affair. Every merchant who attempts, as the saying is, to carry his establishment, finds it no easy task; yet this is what the widow was obliged literally to do. To make her way, thus laden, in the midst of a driving snowstorm was indeed a difficult matter. Half a dozen times she faltered in discouragement. The street led over a steep hill; how was she to reach the top? She struggled along; the wind blew through her thin garments and drove her back; the umbrella bobbed wildly about; her hands grew numb; now the basket, again the camp-seat, kept slipping from her grasp. Several persons passed, but no one seemed to think of stopping to assist her. A party of well-dressed boys were coasting down the middle of the street; what cared they for the storm? Several, who were standing awaiting their turn, glanced idly at the grotesque figure.

"What a guy!" cried Ed Brown, with a laugh, sending a well-aimed snowball straight against the umbrella, which it shook with a thud. He was on the point of following up with another.

"Oh, come!" protested a carelessly good-natured companion. "That's no fun. But here - look out for the other double-runner! Now we go, hurray!"

And, presto, they whizzed by, without another thought of the aged creature toiling up the ascent. No one appeared to have time to help her.

Presently, however, she heard a firm, light step behind her. The next moment a pair of merry brown eyes peered under the umbrella; a face as round and ruddy as one of her best Baldwins beamed upon her with the smile of old friendship, and a gay, youthful voice cried out:

"Good afternoon, Missis Barry! It's hard work getting on to-day, isn't it?"

A singularly gentle expression lighted up the apple-woman's weather-beaten features as she recognized the little fellow in the handsome overcoat, who was evidently returning from an errand, as he carried a milk can in one hand while drawing a sled with the other.

"Indade an' it is, Masther Tom!" she replied, pausing a second.

"Let us see if we can't manage differently," he went on, taking her burden and setting it upon the sled. "There, that is better. Now give me your hand."

She had watched him mechanically; but, thus recalled to

herself, she answered hastily:

"Oh, thank ye kindly, sir! It's too much for ye to be takin' this trouble; but I can get along very well now, with only the umbrelly to carry."

"No trouble at all," said he. "Look, then, - follow me; I'll pick out the best places for you to walk in, - the snow is drifting so!"

He trudged on ahead, glancing back occasionally to see if the basket and camp-seat were safe, or to direct her steps, - as if all this were the most natural thing in the world for him to do, as in truth it was; for, though he thought it a great joke that she should call him "sir," will not any one admit that he deserved the title which belongs to a gentleman? He and Widow Barry had been good friends for some time.

"Sure, an' didn't he buy out me whole supply one day this last January?" she would say. "His birthday it was, and the dear creature was eleven years old. He spent the big silver dollar his grandfather gave him like a prince, a treatin' all the b'ys of the neighborhood to apples an' peanuts, an' sendin' me home to take me comfort."

Tom, moreover, was a regular patron of "the stand." He always declared that "she knew what suited him to a T." During the selection he was accustomed to discuss with her many weighty questions, especially Irish politics, in which they both took a deep if not very well-informed interest.

"Guess I'll have that dark-red one over there. Don't you think Mr. Gladstone is the greatest statesman of the age, Missis Barry? - what? That other one is bigger? Well! - and your father knew Daniel O'Connell you say? - ah, I tell you that's a fine fellow!"

Whether he meant the patriot or the pippin it might be difficult to determine. This, however, is but a specimen of their conversation. Then in the end she would produce the ripest and rosiest of her stock - which she had been keeping for him all the while, - and, leaving a penny in her palm, he would hurry away in order to reach St. Francis' School before the bell rang.

This particular afternoon, when he had helped her over the worst part of the way, she glanced uneasily at the can which he carried, and said:

"Faith, Masther Tom, it's afraid I am that they'll be waitin' at home for the milk ye were sent for. Sure I wouldn't want ye to be blamed for not makin' haste, avick! An' all because of yer doin' a kindly turn for a poor old woman."

"No fear of that, ma'am," answered Tom, confidently. "There is no hurry; the milk won't be needed till supper time."

Then, noticing that she was tired and panting for breath, he took out the stopper and held the can toward her, saying impulsively,

"Have a drink, Missis Barry, - yes, it will do you good."

A suspicious moisture dimmed the widow's faded eyes for a moment, and her heart gave a throb of grateful surprise at the child's ingenuous friendliness; but she drew back with a deprecating gesture, saying,

"Well, well, Masther Tom, ye're the thoughtfullest young gentleman that ever I see! An' I'm sure I thank ye kindly. It isn't for the likes of me to be tellin' ye what is right an' proper, but what would yer mother say to yer not bringin' the milk home just as ye got it from the store, an' to ye givin' a poor creature like me a drink out of the can?"

"Oh, she wouldn't care!" replied Tom. "Didn't she say you were welcome at the house any time, to have a cup of tea and get warm by the kitchen fire? Do you think she'd grudge you a sup of milk?"

"It isn't that; for I know she wouldn't, God bless her!" said the apple-woman, heartily. "Still, asthore, take heed of what I say. Never meddle with what's trusted to ye, but carry it safe an' whole to the person it's meant for, or the place ye are told to fetch it to. It's the best plan, dear."

"I suppose it is, Missis Barry, generally," agreed Tom. "I remember once Ed Brown and I made away with half of a big package of raisins that mother sent me for, and she scolded me about it. But that was different, you know. Pshaw! I didn't mean to tell you it was Ed. Here we are at your door, ma'am. I'll put your things inside - oh, no! Never mind. I was glad to come. Really I oughtn't to take it. Well, thank you. Good-bye!"

And Tom scampered off with an especially toothsome-looking apple, which the woman forced into his hand.

"Ah, but he's the dear, blithe, generous-hearted b'y!" she exclaimed, with a warmth of affectionate admiration, as she stood looking after him. "There's not a bit of worldly pride or meanness about him. May the Lord keep him so! The only thing I'd be afraid of is that, like many such, he'd be easily led. There's that Ed Brown now, - Heaven forgive me, but somehow I don't like that lad. Though he's the son of the richest man in the neighborhood, an' his people live in grand style, he's no fit companion for Masther Tom Norris, I'm thinkin'."

II.

Tom lost no time now in getting home. A little later he had entered a spacious brick house on Florence Street, deposited the milk can on the kitchen table, set the cook a laughing by some droll speech, and, passing on, sought his mother in her cheerful sitting-room.

"Why, my son, what delayed you so long?" she inquired, folding away her sewing; for it was becoming too dark to work.

"Oh, I went home with Missis Barry!" he answered, with the matter-of-fact air with which he might have said that he had been escorting some particular friend of the family.

Mrs. Norris smiled and drew nearer to the bright fire which burned in the grate. Tom slipped into a seat beside her upon the wide, old-fashioned sofa, which was just the place for one of those cosy twilight chats with mother, which boys especially love so much, and the memory of which gleams, star-like, through the mists of years, exerting even far greater influence than she dreams of upon their lives. Tom considered this quiet half hour the pleasantest of the day. Mrs. Norris, with a gentle wisdom worthy of wider imitation, encouraged him to talk to her about whatever interested him. She was seldom too tired or too preoccupied at this time to hear of the mechanism of the steam-engine, the mysteries of the printing-press, or the feats that may be performed with a bicycle, - of which "taking a header," or the method by which the rider learns to fly off the machine head foremost into a ditch with impunity, appeared to be the most desirable. Her patience in this respect was rewarded by that most precious possession to a mother, a son's confidence.

Tom liked to tell her of various things that happened during the day; to compare notes, and get her opinions of matters in general; at the same time giving his own, which were often quaint and entertaining.

"Really, mother, Missis Barry knows a lot!" he now exclaimed, abruptly, clasping his knee and staring at the fire in a meditative manner.

Mrs. Norris looked amused, but she did not venture to question the apple-vender's wisdom. One or two kindly inquiries about the old woman, however, prompted him to speak of her further, - of his meeting her as she struggled along with her burden, his drawing it on the sled, and last of her refusal of the drink he offered.

"You would not have minded, would you, mother?" he asked.

"No, not for the sake of the milk, certainly," responded Mrs. Norris, laughing; "but -" then she hesitated. How could she hamper the mind of this ingenuous little lad of hers with false and finical ideas of refinement and delicacy! Why should she suggest to him that it is at least not customary to go about giving the poor to drink out of our own especial milk cans? There came to her mind the noble lines which but frame as with jewels the simple Christian precept, - the words spoken to Sir Launfal when, weary, poverty-stricken, and disheartened, the knight returns from his fruitless search for the Holy Grail; when humbly he shares his cup and crust with the leper at the gate, - the leper who straightway stands before him glorified, a vision of Our Lord, and tells him that true love of our neighbor consists in,

"Not what we give, but what we share;
For the gift without the giver is bare."

And then the mother's hands rested lovingly a moment upon Tom's head, as again she repeated more softly: "No, certainly."

*   *   *   *   *

As Widow Barry had surmised, the keynote of Tom's nature was that he was easily led, and therein rested the possibilities of great good or evil. The little confidential chats with his mother were a strong safeguard to him, and laid the foundation of the true principles by which he should be guided; but, as he mingled more with other boys, he was not always steadfast in acting up to his knowledge of what was right, and was apt to be more influenced by his companions than his best friends cared to see him. At present he was inclined to make a chum of Ed Brown, who, though only a year older, was so precociously shrewd, and what the world calls "smart," that, according to good Widow Barry's opinion, "he could buy and sell Masther Tom any day."

The old woman had, indeed, many opportunities for observation; for is not sometimes so simple a transaction as the buying of an apple a real test of character? If a boy or man is tricky or mean or unjust in his business dealings, is it likely that we shall find him upright and honorable in other things? Though Mrs. Norris was not as well posted as the apple-vender, one or two occurrences had caused her to positively forbid Tom to have any more to do with Ed, - a command which he grumbled a good deal about, and, alas! occasionally disobeyed.

But to continue our story. The following Saturday morning the skies were blue, the sun shone bright, the gladness of spring was in the air, - all promised a long, pleasant holiday. The apple stand at the corner had a prosperous aspect. The umbrella, though shabbier and more rakish-looking than ever, wore a cheery, hail-fellow-well-met appearance. Widow Barry had, as she told a neighbor, "spruced up her old bonnet a bit," - an evidence of the approach of spring, which the boys recognized and appreciated. Now she was engaged in polishing up her apples, and arranging the peanuts as invitingly as possible; a number of pennies already jingled in the small bag attached to her apron-string, in which she kept her money.

"Ah, here comes Masther Tom!" she exclaimed, presently. "An' right glad I am; for he always brings me a good hansel."

"Hello, Missis Barry!" cried he. "How's trade to-day? Too early to tell yet? Well, see if I can't boom it a little. Give me a dozen apples, and one - yes, two quarts of nuts."

Pleased and flustered at this stroke of fortune, she busied herself in getting out two of the largest of her paper bags, and filling the munificent order. But Tom was not like himself this morning. He had plenty to say, to be sure; but he talked away with a kind of reckless gaiety that appeared a trifle forced, and he was eager to be off.

The old woman paused a second, as if suddenly impressed by the difference in his manner; then, by a shake of the head, she strove to banish the thought, which she reproached herself for as an unworthy suspicion, and smiled as if to reassure herself. With a pleasant word she put the well-filled bags into Tom's hands, and received the silver he offered in payment - three bright new dimes. At that moment she caught a glimpse of Ed Brown lurking in the area way of a house at the other end of the block. The sight filled her with a vague misgiving which she could not have explained. She glanced again at Tom; he was nervous and excited.

"Wait a bit," said she, laying a restraining hand upon his arm.

"What is the matter? Didn't I give you just the price?" he inquired, somewhat impatiently.

The old woman bent forward and peered anxiously into his face; her kind but searching eyes seemed to look down into his very soul, as, in a voice trembling with emotion, she replied: "Yes: but tell me, asthore, where did ye get the money?"

Tom's countenance changed; he tried to put her off, saying, "Pshaw! Why do you want to ask a fellow such a question? Haven't I bought more than this of you before?"

"Troth an' ye have, dear; but not in this way, I'm thinkin'," she answered.

"It's all right. Do let me go, Missis Barry!" cried he, vexed and beginning to feel decidedly frightened.

"Hi, Tom, come on!" called Ed Brown, emerging from the area.

"Look here, Masther Tom, darlin'! You'll not move a step with them things, an' I'll not put up that money till I know where it came from."

"Well, then," said Tom, doggedly, seeing that escape was impossible, "I got it at home, off the mantel in the sitting-room."

"Oh, yes!" ejaculated Mrs. Barry, raising her eyes toward heaven, as if praying for the pardon of the offence.

"Why, that's nothing!" he went on. "Ed Brown says lots of boys do it. Some take the change out of their father's pockets even, if they get a chance. His father don't mind a bit. He always has plenty of cash, Ed has."

"Ah, yes, that ne'er-do-well, Ed Brown!" said the old woman, shaking her fist at the distant Ed, who, realizing that Tom had got into trouble, disappeared in a twinkling.

"An' his father don't mind! Then it's because he knows nothin' about it. They'll come a day of reckonin' for him. An' you -"

"Oh, the folks at home won't care!" persisted Tom, thoroughly ashamed, but still anxious to excuse himself. "Mother always says that everything in the house is for the use of the family. If we children should make a raid on the pantry, and carry off a pie or cake, she might punish us for the disobedience, but she wouldn't call it stealing." He blushed as he uttered the ugly word.

"Yes, but to take money is different, ye know," continued his relentless mentor, whose heart, however, was sorrowing over

MARY CATHERINE CROWLEY

him with the tenderness of a mother for her child.

Tom was silent; he did know, had really known from the first, though now his fault stood before him in its unsightliness; all the pretexts by which he had attempted to palliate it fell from it like a veil, and showed the hateful thing it was. He could not bring himself to acknowledge it, however. Sullenly he set down the apples and peanuts, murmuring, "I never did it before, anyhow!"

"No, nor never will again, I'm sure, avick! This'll be a lifelong lesson to ye," returned the old woman, with agitation, as she put the dimes back into his hand. "Go right home with them now, an' tell yer father all about it."

"My father!" faltered Tom, doubtful of the consequences of such a confession.

"Well, yer mother, then. She'll be gentle with ye, never fear, if ye are really sorry."

"Indeed I am, Missis Barry," declared Tom, quite breaking down at last.

"I'm certain ye are, asthore!" continued the good creature, heartily. "An', whisper, when ye get home go to yer own little room, an' there on yer bended knees ask God to forgive ye. Make up yer mind to shun bad company for the future; an' never, from this hour, will we speak another word about this - either ye to me or I to ye, - save an' except ye may come an' say: 'I've done as ye bid me, Missis Barry. It's all hunkey dory!'"

The old woman smiled with grim humor as she found herself quoting the boy's favorite slang expression.

Tom laughed in spite of himself, so droll did it sound from her lips; but at the same time he drew his jacket sleeve across his eyes, which had grown strangely dim, and said:

"I will, Missis Barry. You may trust me: I will."

And Tom did. From that day he and the honest old apple-woman were better friends than ever. Meanwhile her trade improved so much that before long she was able to set up a more pretentious establishment, - a genuine stand, with an awning to replace the faithful umbrella, which was forthwith honorably retired from service. Here she carried on a thriving business for several years, Tom, though now a student at St. Jerome's College, often bought apples and peanuts of her.

"You see that old woman?" said he to a comrade one day. "Don't look much like an angel, does she?"

His friend, glancing at the queer figure and plain, ordinary features, was amused at the comparison.

"And yet," continued Tom, earnestly, "she proved a second Guardian Angel to me once, and I'll bless her all my life for it."

MARY CATHERINE CROWLEY

"BETTER THAN RICHES"

I.

"Cash! Cash! here!" cried an attendant at the stationery counter of one of New York's great shopping emporiums. At the summons a delicate-looking little girl came wearily up, and held out a small wicker basket for the goods and the money. "Be quick now: the lady's in a hurry."

Notwithstanding the injunction, the child started off with no special attempt at haste. The same words were dinned into her ears a hundred times a day. She did not see why ladies should be in a hurry. The ladies of her world seemed to have nothing to do but to wear pretty clothes, and to shop, which meant principally the buying of more pretty clothes. It was all very well to make an extra effort to oblige one occasionally; but if she did it every time she was exhorted to, surely her tired feet would give out before the end of the day.

"Cash is so poky!" complained the salesgirl to her companion behind the counter.

"Hie you, Cash! Hustle I say!" called the floor-walker peremptorily, as he passed.

Thus warned, the child skurried away, and reappeared after a very brief interval. As she rushed up with the parcel, an awkward accident occurred. The lady heedlessly stepped backward. Cash dodged; but, alas! before she could stop herself, she had dashed into a pyramid of note-paper that stood upon the end of the counter, and sent the boxes scattering over the floor in dire confusion.

"Oh! - oh, my!" exclaimed the salesgirl, distressed, as she contemplated the wreck of the architectural display.

The disturbance at once brought the floor-walker to the spot. "Stupid!" he muttered, taking poor Cash by the shoulder. "Why don't you look where you're going? If you can't mind what you're about, we have no use for you here; remember that!"

"Please do not blame the child," interposed the lady who had unwittingly caused the trouble. "It was my fault: I carelessly got in her way. I am very sorry."

"Don't mention it, Mrs. M --. It is not of the slightest consequence," said the floor-walker, with a bland smile and a bow. (Mrs. M - was a desirable customer, and he would have said the same thing if she had happened to tip the show-case over.) "We have to keep our employees up to the mark, you know," he added in a low tone, by way of apology for his brusqueness. "The best of them become careless. But Cash has found a friend this time, so we'll let it pass."

Cash, who was busily picking up the boxes, made a little grimace to herself at his change of manner. The lady politely inclined her head by way of acknowledgment, and the floor-walker left abruptly, having suddenly discovered that something required his immediate attention in another part of the store.

When he had disappeared, the little girl looked up and faltered gratefully: "Thank you, ma'am!"

Mrs. M - now for the first time took notice of the individual to whom she had just rendered a service. She glanced down upon a freckled face of the complexion described as pasty, a pair of greyish-blue eyes, and a tangle of reddish curls just long enough to admit of being tied back with the bit of crumpled ribbon which kept them tidy. Cash was not of prepossessing appearance; yet perhaps because, the grateful glance touched a chord common to humanity in the heart of the stranger, or because one naturally warms to any creature whom one has befriended, or perhaps simply from the sweet womanliness which finds all childhood attractive, - whatever the motive, upon the impulse of the moment the lady did a very graceful thing. Taking a rose from the bunch of jacqueminots she wore, she fastened it to the breast of the child's black apron, and was gone before the latter could recover from her astonishment.

It was only a little incident, but it changed the whole aspect of Cash's day. The beautiful flower glowed against the dark uniform, like a bit of joy vouchsafed to a sombre life.

"How lovely!" exclaimed the salesgirl. "Aren't you lucky, Cash! Don't you want to exchange with me? I'll give you a delicious orange I brought with my lunch for that posie."

Cash shook her head. As soon as she could, she stole away to the room where the girls kept their cloaks and hats. Here, after a furtive look around to see that ho one was by who might snatch, it away, she unpinned the rose and slipped it into a small card-board box, having first carefully wrapped the stem in a piece of well moistened paper. Then she tucked the box into the pocket of her jacket, and ran downstairs to the store again.

For the next two or three hours it happened that Cash was kept running to and fro almost without intermission; but she did not mind it now. The kindly word spoken in her behalf by the truly gracious lady, the simple gift of a flower, had given her new spirit. Her heart, like a little bird, kept singing a cheery song to itself; while, as she journeyed hither and thither, her feet seemed to keep time to its gladness.

"Why, Cash, you're getting smart! What has waked you up?" said the salesgirl, when, well on in the afternoon, the child sat down by the counter for a few seconds. Then, without waiting for a reply, she continued: "Now, aren't you sorry you did not exchange with me? See, you've lost your rose!"

"Oh, 'taint losted," answered the girl.

"You did not give it to any one after I made the first bid?" (The inquiry was in a sharper tone.)

"No: I'm keeping it for Ellie."

"Oh, sure enough! Poor Ellie! how is she? Cash, you're a good little thing to remember her so kindly. Here, I have the orange still; take it to her, too."

The child's eyes sparkled with pleasure as the salesgirl put the golden ball into her hand. "Ellie'll be awful pleased. I'll tell her you sent it, Julia," she said.

Cash had, of course, another name: it was Katy Connors. Katy lived way over on the east side of the city, in a house which was once a handsome dwelling, but had long since been divided into tenements and given up to ruin. The Connors were known among their neighbors as a respectable, hard-working family. The father was a day-laborer; the mother went out washing; Joe, a boy of fourteen, was in the district messenger service; after him came Katy, who was employed in McNaughton's store; and then Ellie, the little invalid. Two younger children had died in infancy.

Poor Ellie was fast becoming helpless. How different it had been a few months before! What a sturdy, active, child she was, when one morning she set out in gay spirits "to earn money for mother!" Like Katy, she had obtained a position as cashgirl in McNaughton's. And how quick and smart she was about her duties! The floor-walker commended her twice during the week, and said he would speak for an increase in her wages. How proud she felt when Saturday came, and she knew she would have two dollars and a half to take home! Unfortunately, it was to be dearly gained.

MARY CATHERINE CROWLEY

Saturday afternoon it happened that the store was unusually crowded; everything was stir and confusion. Little Ellie and her companions dashed now here, now there, in response to the unceasing cry of "Cash! Cash!" In the midst of the hurry, the floor-walker gave Ellie a message to deliver to one of the clerks in the basement. "Don't delay!" he called after her. Eager to please, the child made her way through the throng, and was on the point of darting down the stairs, when, alas! her foot caught, she tripped, gave a little scream, and was precipitated down the entire flight. In an instant several employees from the neighboring counters rushed to pick her up; but, to their alarm, though she strove to be brave, when they attempted to move her she could not repress a low moan of anguish. The superintendent sent at once for a doctor, who discovered that she had sustained a severe injury, having struck against the edge of one of the iron steps.

Where was now the proud home-coming? Ellie was taken to the hospital, whither frightened Mrs. Connors was summoned. Upon one of the cots in the accident ward lay the child, her small face wan with pain, and in her eyes the startled expression noticeable in those of a person who has had a serious fall. In one feverish hand she held something tightly clasped - something for which she had asked before being carried from the store. When the doctor turned aside she beckoned to her mother, and, with a pathetic little smile, folded into the palm of the weeping woman a small yellow envelope. The next moment she fainted away, Mrs. Connors' tears flowed faster as she beheld the precious offering - Ellie's first wages, and the last which she was likely ever to earn.

The firm of McNaughton & Co. investigated the accident, to see if they could by any means be liable to an action for damages brought by an employee. But there was no loose nail in the stairway, not the least obstruction. The proprietors were not to blame; it was simply the child's heedlessness, they said. In fact, the fault was with Ellie's shoes: the sole of one, being broken, caught on the top step and caused her fall.

And she was to have had a new pair that very evening. Mrs. Connors had quietly determined that her first earnings should be expended in this way. Poor Ellie! she would not need shoes now: the doctors feared she would never walk again. The firm sent a twenty-dollar bill to the child's mother, another "Cash" was engaged to take Ellie's place, and the matter was speedily forgotten.

II.

Not growing better at the hospital, Ellie begged to be taken home. Rather than live apart from those she loved, she strove to be content to remain alone day after day, propped up by an inverted chair upon a wretched bed. Or, when she felt stronger, with the aid of a pair of rude crutches, she would drag herself to the window to watch patiently for the return of the dear bread-winners, whose toil she would so willingly have shared.

There, in a little stuffy room, upon the top floor of the old house, she spent the long, sultry summer; there she remained when autumn came; there the approaching Christmas holidays were likely to find her.

How was it, then, that Ellie was generally cheery and blithe? Perhaps her mother's prayer each morning, as she bade her good-bye to go to work, had most to do with it. "May Jesus and His Blessed Mother watch over you, mavourneen!" the good woman would say, with a sigh at the necessity for leaving her.

Frequently, when the child could have wept for loneliness, the words would keep echoing in her heart. She was a well-disposed little creature, and those hours spent alone often brought serious thoughts, which molded and beautified her character. But Ellie was a thoroughly natural child: there was none of the story-book goodness about her. She was keenly interested in everything that went on. She thought there was no one like mother, but it was Katy who represented the world to her, - the world of McNaughton's store, with its brightness and beautiful wares, and its ever-changing crowd of handsomely costumed ladies intent upon the pleasures of shopping. Any scrap of news which one fagged out little cashgirl brought home at the close of the day was eagerly listened to by the other; who found her enforced idleness so irksome.

Katy had a great deal to narrate at the close of the day upon which our story opened. Sitting upon the foot of Ellie's bed, she told how she upset the pyramid of note-paper; and what trouble she would have been in, but for the kind lady who so promptly came to the rescue. To Ellie's quick imagination the story had all the charm of a fairy tale. And when, at the close, her sister placed in her hands the orange and the tiny box wherein lay the rose, still quite fresh and fragrant, her face beamed with delight; and Katy went to bed very happy, feeling herself more than repaid for having treasured them so carefully.

The next morning, when Katy reached the store, she found everybody in a state of pleasurable excitement over the opening of the holiday goods; for it wanted but three weeks to Christmas. At the end of the stationery counter, where the pyramid of note-paper had been, an immense stack of dolls was now attractively displayed. The little cashgirl stood before it, lost in admiration. There were little dolls and big ones; dolls with blue eyes, and others with brown; some with light hair, and some with dark; *bebee Jumeau* and *bebee Brue*; rubber dolls, and rag dolls with *papier-mache* faces.

"How lovely they are!" she murmured to herself, including even the plainest and least among them in her appreciation of the gorgeous company. "Don't I wish Ellie could see them!" she continued. "I'll have to count them, so as to tell her how many there are; for I don't believe that by herself she could imagine such a lot of dolls together."

Katy and Ellie had never had a doll in their lives, - that is, a real *boughten* one, as they called those not of home manufacture.

The kind salesgirl who had sent the orange to Ellie, from her post behind the counter, noticed the child's wonderment.

"Will you look at Cash!" she said to a companion. Katy was oblivious of them, however. After watching her a few moments, Julia called out:

"Well, Cash, which do you like best?"

The little girl looked the dolls over again with much deliberation; and finally, pointing to a good-sized one, with golden hair and large eyes, said:

"This."

"Oh, one of those ninety-seven cent dolls!" responded Julia. "They *are* handsome for the price. Sawdust bodies, to be sure; but what fine heads? - red cheeks, splendid eyes, and hair that will comb out as well as that of some costlier ones, I'll be bound."

"Ninety-seven cents!" repeated Katy, with a sigh. It was an unattainable sum, as far as she was concerned. The salesgirl remarked the sigh.

"Say, Cash, why don't you buy it?" she urged. "Your mother'll let you keep part of your wages for yourself Christmas week, won't she? And you wouldn't get such another bargain in a doll if you hunted a year and a day. You'd better speak for it quick, though; for when the rush of trade comes, there's no knowing how long the lot will last."

Katy shook her head. "I wouldn't want to buy a Christmas present for myself," she answered. "But I was wishing - only there is really no use in wishing; still, just supposing there was - I was thinking if I could only get that doll for Ellie, how happy she would be. You know she has to be alone so much, and she gets awful blue sometimes; though she won't let on, 'cause it would fret mother. But the doll would be great company for her. We've neither of us ever had one."

She continued to gaze longingly at the rosy beauty, while the salesgirl meditatively dusted the show-case.

"Stop! I'll tell you how you can manage to get it," Julia said, suddenly. "It's the rule of this store that on Christmas Eve, after all the customers are gone, each employee may choose as a present from the firm some article worth a quarter of his or her wages for the week. Let's see: you're paid three dollars, aren't you?"

Katy nodded.

"That would count for seventy-five cents on the doll; then all you would have to put to it would be twenty-two cents. Couldn't you do that somehow?"

"Yes!" cried Katy, delighted. "Sometimes I run errands for a dressmaker who lives in the block below us, and she gives me pennies, or once in a while a nickel. And when my aunt's husband comes to see us - he's a widder man and sorter rich; he drives a truck, - well, when he comes 'casionally, he gives each of us children as much as ten cents; and I guess he'll be round about Christmas time. Oh, yes, I'm almost sure I can make up the twenty-two cents!"

"But, then, when the doll is yours, won't you hate to give it away?" queried Julia; for Katy already began to assume an air of possession.

"Oh, not to Ellie! And, you know, she'll be sure to let me hold it sometimes" was the ingenuous reply.

The quick tears sprang to the salesgirl's eyes, and she turned abruptly away, to arrange some dolls upon the shelves behind her.

"After all, love is better than riches," she reflected, as the picture of the crippled child in the humble home arose in her mind, and she gave a sidelong glance at Katy's thin face and shabby dress.

"You will be sure to save this very doll for me, won't you?" pleaded the child.

MARY CATHERINE CROWLEY

"I can't put it aside for you," she explained, "because the floor-walker would not allow that; but I'll arrange so you will have one of the lot, never fear."

"But I want this one," declared Katy.

"My goodness gracious, you foolish midget! They're all as much alike as rows of peas in a pod," exclaimed her friend, a trifle impatiently.

"No," insisted the little girl. "All the others have red painted buckles on their shoes, but this doll has blue buckles; and I'm sure Ellie would prefer blue buckles, 'cause we've often talked about it when we played choosing what we'd like best."

"Well, well!" laughed Julia. "All right, Katy: I'll save it, if I can."

Satisfied by this promise, the child ran away; for customers began to come in, and to loiter would be to lessen her chance of gaining the treasure which to herself she already called Ellie's.

McNaughton & Co. did a great business within the next two weeks; the employees were "fearfully rushed," as they expressed it. Katy had no opportunity for further conversation with the sociable attendant at the end of the stationery counter, now given over to toys, upon the subject oftenest in her thoughts. She had been transferred to another department; but every day she took occasion to go around and look at the doll, to make sure that it was still there; and the kindly salesgirl always found time to give her an encouraging nod and a smile.

One afternoon, however, a few days before Christmas, when Julia returned from her lunch she met Katy, who was crying bitterly. The cause of her distress was soon told. A new girl had been put at the counter that morning; she knew nothing about Katy's doll, and now, as luck would have it, was just in the act of selling it to a big, bluff-looking man, who said he wanted it for his little daughter.

Julia rushed to her post. The man was upon the point of paying for the doll, and had decided that he would take the parcel with him.

"Have you seen the brown-eyed dolls?" she interposed, pleasantly. The other girl scowled at the interference with 'her sale,' but she persisted. "The brown-eyed ones are considered the most desirable."

"Are they?" the man hesitated. "Well, I believe I'll take one, then, instead of this. My little maid likes brown eyes."

Katy's doll was saved. The child, in a fever of suspense, had watched the transaction from behind a pile of dry-goods. Now she turned toward her friend a face bright with gratitude, as she hurried away in response to the imperative call of "Cash."

When Julia recovered from her flurry, she explained matters to her associate. The girl's ill-humor quickly vanished once she understood the situation, and she willingly agreed to help retain the doll if possible.

III

On the morning of the day before Christmas, Katy appeared at the counter and offered the twenty-two cents which she had succeeded in getting together - the balance to be paid on her present.

"Can't I take the doll now, please?" she begged.

"You will have to ask the floor-walker," replied Julia.

She did so, but he said she must wait until evening; he could not make any exceptions. So she was obliged to control her impatience.

Scarcely five minutes afterward a crash was heard. The equilibrium of the rack of dolls had been disturbed, and the whole collection was dashed to the floor. Fortunately, only three or four of the dolls were broken; but, alas! among them was the one Katy had set her heart upon giving to her sick sister.

The commotion brought her to the scene at once. Poor Katy! She did not burst out crying, as Julia expected; but just clasped her hands and stood looking at the wreck of the doll, with an expression of hopeless disappointment, which would have seemed ludicrous, considering the cause, had it not been so pathetic. It aroused the ready sympathy of Julia.

"Don't feel so bad, midget!" she whispered, picking up the pieces. "See: only the head is spoiled. There's another with the feet knocked off. I'll get permission to take the two dolls up to the toy-mender's room, and have the head of the other put on your doll; that will make it as good as new."

When order was restored, she made her request of the floor-walker.

"All right," he answered. "It will cut down the loss by

ninety-seven cents; so you may have it done, if they can spare the time upstairs. That is an awkward corner, anyhow; it will have to be left free in future."

At noon Julia snatched a few moments from the short interval allowed her to get her lunch, and hurried up to the toy-mender's quarters. She prevailed upon him to have the doll repaired in the course of an hour or two; he promised to do so, and it was sent back to her early in the afternoon.

That day Katy's duties, fortunately for her peace of mind, brought her frequently into the vicinity of the doll counter. Now she hastened to it, in a quiver of excitement, to witness the success of the process. When the cover was taken off the box, her cheeks crimsoned with indignation and her eyes blazed, as she turned inquiringly to Julia.

"Indeed, Katy, it is none of my doings," protested the salesgirl; though the result of the experiment was so funny she had not the heart to laugh. The doll with the beautiful blue buckles on her shoes had now a mop of darky wool, and a face as black as the ace of spades.

Julia's quick wit at once jumped at the correct conclusion regarding the apparent blunder. The toy-mender's two thoughtless apprentices had played a joke upon the little cashgirl.

"It is only the nonsense of those rogues upstairs. I'll take the doll back and tell them they must fix it to-night, or I'll complain of them for their fooling at this busy time," she announced, energetically; for she noted the twitching around the corners of Katy's mouth, notwithstanding the child's brave effort at self-control.

Katy went off partially comforted.

"It's mean to tease a child in that way," added Julia, in an audible aside, as she laid the doll on the shelf behind, and wished that the lady to whom she was showing some very handsome dolls would finish her choice, so that she might get a free minute to run up to the mending room again. But the interest of the customer had been awakened by the little drama enacted before her.

"What is the matter?" she inquired, cordially.

Julia looked disconcerted; but the lady had such a sweet and noble face, and her manner was so winning, that the girl found herself telling briefly not only the history of Katy's doll, but of Katy and Ellie too. It was not a waste of time either; for while she talked the purchaser made one or two additional selections, and then, after giving directions concerning them, passed on.

"Do you know who that was?" asked Katy, rushing up as the lady turned into another aisle of the store.

"Yes: Mrs. M -, of 34th Street. Of course she left her address for the parcels," replied Julia.

"It's my Rose-lady, as I call her, - don't you remember the one who gave me the pretty flower?" cried the child.

"Why, so it is!" rejoined Julia. "Well, she's a lovely lady certainly. She happened to ask what the trouble was about the doll; and was so interested I couldn't help telling how you had saved and planned to get it for Ellie, and all about it."

"Mercy! did you?" answered the child, in confusion. "My, but you're the talker, Julia! What would the likes of her care to hear about that!"

The store kept open till half-past eleven Christmas Eve; but at length the last customer was gone, and the employees were allowed to choose their presents. Katy skipped around with joy when the doll was put into her arms. After a moment, however, Julia whisked it away again, and sent it to be packed in a box. The box proved to be large and clumsy, but this was accounted for upon the plea of haste.

"Well, good-night and merry Christmas, Julia!" said the little cashgirl, gratefully. "I don't know how to thank you enough for being so good, and helping me so much, - indeed I don't!"

"Never mind trying," answered Julia, brightly, but with an earnestness unusual to her. "Isn't this Christmas Eve, and didn't the Infant Jesus come to help us, and teach us to do what we can for one another? Just say a prayer for me at Mass to-morrow; that is all I ask."

"You may be sure I will," Katy responded, heartily.

"Good-night! Merry Christmas to you all, and especially to Ellie!" added Julia, hurrying away.

Katy's father was waiting for her at one of the entrances of the store. After a slight demur, she allowed him to carry the package, while she trudged along at his side. The stores were closed, the gay throng of shoppers had disappeared. People were still abroad upon the great thoroughfares; but the side streets were deserted, except when, now and again, overtaxed workers like herself were to be met making their way home. The lamps burned dim, save where, occasionally, an electric light flared up with a spectral glare. The glitter of the world had departed. It was past midnight; in the deep blue of the winter's sky the stars glowed with a peaceful radiance. Looking up at them, Katy began to think, in her own simple fashion, of the meaning of Christmas and of Christmas gifts; of Bethlehem, the Virgin Mother, and the Divine Child; of the Love that came into the world on that holy night of long ago, to kindle in all hearts a spirit of kindliness and helpfulness toward one another, making it more blessed to give than to receive. The little girl realized the happiness of making others happy, when she handed to Ellie the bulky package over which she had kept watch all the way to the house.

The usually pale face of the young invalid flushed with excitement, while, with trembling fingers, she unfastened the wrappings and opened the box.

"O Katy!" she exclaimed, as she beheld the hard-won present, - "O Katy!" It was all she could say, but the tone and the look which accompanied it were quite enough.

At first neither of the children could think of anything besides the doll; but after a while Ellie made another discovery. As she trifled with the box, she cried:

"Why, there's something else here!"

The next moment she drew out a doll precisely like the first, except that its shoes had red buckles; at the sight of which Katy immediately concluded that, for herself, she liked red buckles better. Attached to it was a card on which was written: "For an unselfish little sister."

"It did not get there by mistake: it's for you, Katy," said Ellie, ecstatically.

"Then the Rose-lady must have sent it," declared Katy, feeling as if she were in a dream.

That her conjecture was correct was evident the next day; for about noon a carriage stopped at the door of the dilapidated house in - street; and a visitor, who seemed to bring with her an additional share of Christmas sunshine, was shown up to the Connors' tenement. She was followed by a tall footman, who quietly deposited upon the table a generous basket of the season's delicacies.

"The Rose-lady, mother!" cried Katy, pinching her own arm to see if she could possibly be awake.

It was all true, however; and that day the Connors family found a devoted friend. Henceforth the Rose-lady took a special interest in Ellie. She induced a celebrated doctor to go and see her. The great man said there was a chance that the crippled child might be cured by electricity; and it was arranged that the mother should take her regularly to his office for treatment, Mrs. M - offering the use of her carriage.

Now Ellie can walk almost as well as ever. She is growing stronger every day, and will probably before long be able to attain her ambition - "to earn money to help mother."

"And to think, Katy," the little girl often says, affectionately, "it all came about through your wanting to give me that Christmas doll!"

BUILDING A BOAT

I.

"Oh, if we only had a boat, what jolly fun we might have!" exclaimed Jack Gordon regretfully, following with his eyes the bright waters as they rushed along, - now coursing smoothly, now leaping in the sunshine; again darkened for the moment, and eddying beneath the shade of the overhanging branches of a willow tree; then in the distance coming almost to a standstill, and expanding into the clear, floating mirror of the mill-pond.

"That's so," answered Rob Stuart, laconically. The two boys were lounging on the bank of the creek, which, though dignified by the name of Hohokus River and situated in New Jersey, is not considered of sufficient importance to be designated on the map of that State, even by one of those wavering, nameless lines which seem to be hopelessly entangled with one another for the express purpose of confusing a fellow who has neglected his geography lesson until the last moment.

"Yes, if we had a boat we might explore this stream from source to mouth," continued Jack, who was always in search of adventures.

"A canoe?" suggested Rob.

"That would be just the thing," agreed Jack. "But a regular canoe, made of birch bark or paper, would cost too much. I'll tell you what it is, Rob. Jim and I have next to nothing in the treasury at present. We haven't had a chance to earn much lately."

"I'm about dead broke, too," replied Rob.

"I say," exclaimed Jack, after a moment of silence, "suppose we make one?"

"Make one!" echoed Rob, surprised.

"Why, yes. All we need is a flat-bottomed boat; and it ought not to be hard to put one together. Uncle Gerald promised to give me some boards for my chicken-coops; perhaps he would add a few more if he knew what we wanted them for. Let's go over and see if he is at home now,"

"All right," answered Rob, preparing to start.

Jack and Rob might almost always be found together. They were of about the same age, - Jack being fourteen on his last birthday, the 22d of January, and Rob on the 30th of the following March. They lived within a stone's-throw of each other, and had been friends from the time they were little chaps.

Mr. Gerald Sheridan was a merchant who did business in New York, but he was now taking a few days' vacation, to look a little after the work upon his farm, which was in charge of a hired man. His house, situated a short distance down the road, was large and spacious. The boys walked briskly toward it, planning as they went.

At Uncle Gerald's the latch string was always out - that is, if the door was not standing hospitably open, as was usually the case in pleasant spring or summer weather; one had only to turn the knob and walk in. Just as they were about to enter the square, home-like hall, lined with old-fashioned settles and adorned with fowling-pieces, fishing-rods, tennis rackets, and the like, Jack's cousin, eleven-year-old Leo, came out of an adjoining room and said;

"Hello! You want to see father? Well, he's over yonder" -
pointing to a sunny patch of ground toward the south, -
"showing Michael how he wants the vegetable garden planted.
Wait a minute and I'll go with you."

Leo's hat having been discovered in a corner where he had
tossed it an hour or two earlier, they started on a race to the
garden, and brought up suddenly in front of Uncle Gerald,
who now, in a dark blue flannel shirt, trousers to match, and a
broad-brimmed hat of grey felt, was evidently dressed for the
role of a farmer. He was a pleasant man, tall and slight in
figure, with blue eyes, a brown beard, and a cheery, kindly
manner, which made him a favorite with everybody, and
especially with boys, in whose projects he was always
interested.

"Give you the wood to build a boat?" he repeated, when told
what Jack and Rob wanted to accomplish. "Willingly. I am
glad to have you attempt something of the kind. I have always
maintained that boys should be taught to work with their
hands. Every youth ought to learn the use of tools, just as a girl
learns to sew, to cook, and help her mother in household
duties. Then we should not have so many awkward, stupid,
bungling fellows, who can not do anything for themselves. It is
as disgraceful for a lad not to be able to drive a nail straight
without pounding his fingers or thumb as it is for a girl not to
know how to stitch on a button. But I am letting my hobby
run away with me, and no doubt you are anxious to be off.
You will find the lumber piled in the storeroom of the barn.
Take what you need. Perhaps Leo will lend you his pony to
draw the load home."

"Thank you, sir!" answered Jack, heartily.

Now that the means of carrying out his plan were insured to
him, he did not feel in such a hurry; and, furthermore, though
quite satisfied that he should have no trouble about it, he

would not have objected to a few hints as to how to begin.

"Can you tell me, Uncle," asked the boy, half jocosely, "if any of the distinguished men you are thinking of ever attempted to make a boat?"

"To be sure," returned the gentleman. "There was Peter the Great, who, though a tyrannical ruler, might have earned fair wages as a ship-builder. But we shall have to talk about him another time, when I have leisure; for I see that at present Michael wants me to devote all my attention to tomato plants, peas, beans, and seed potatoes. If you wait till tomorrow, I will show you how to set to work."

"Oh, I guess we can get on!" returned Jack, becoming impatient again, and feeling that it would be impossible to delay, with the whole bright day before them. Rob seemed to be of the same opinion.

Uncle Gerald smiled, reflecting that, since manual training does not begin with boat-building, they would soon discover the task so confidently undertaken to be a far greater one than they realized. He made no comment, however; and the boys started for the barn-loft, where they selected the wood best suited to their purpose, and carried it down to the yard, where Leo had dragged out the pony wagon.

"Here," said he, "you may stow the boards into this; and I'll lend you Winkie to draw them home, if you'll promise to let Jim and me see you build the boat."

Jack's brother Jim was a year older than Leo; but the two chummed together, and were accustomed to stand up for each other, and thus hold their own against the big boys, who were sometimes rather too much inclined to adopt a patronizing tone toward them.

Jack and Rob now exchanged significant glances, which said plainly that they would prefer the loan of the pony without

MARY CATHERINE CROWLEY

any conditions. It would be annoying to have the little fellows "tagging after them." But there was no help for it. The pony belonged to Leo, and they could not take it without his permission.

"Oh - ahem - I suppose so! Hey, Rob?" said Jack, shutting one eye expressively.

"Well - yes," agreed Rob, appreciating the situation.

They went round to the front of Winkie's stall. Immediately a shaggy head protruded through the window-like opening, a pair of bright eyes passed over the other visitors and rested upon Leo, with a look which might well be interpreted as one of affection; and a rough nose rubbed up against the boy's arm, this being Winkle's way of expressing delight at seeing his master. He rather resented any attempt at petting from Jack or Rob, however; which led them to tease him, much as they would play with a dog, - for he was only a little Shetland pony, hardly larger than a good-sized Newfoundland.

"Kittelywink!" exclaimed Rob, giving him his full name, which had been shortened for the sake of euphony. "What in the world did you call him that for?"

"Well, I can't exactly say," replied Leo; "but somehow it's a name that's all jumbled up and confused like, and, that is just about how you feel when he gets playing his pranks. Presto, change! you know. Now you're here, and now you don't know where you are, but most likely it is in the middle of a dusty or muddy road. Oh, you don't mind the fall, 'cause he has an accommodating way of letting you down easy; but it hurts your feelings awful, especially if there's anybody round. You don't seem as big as you were a few moments before. He doesn't act that way with me now, because I try to be always kind and gentle with him. But you just attempt to really plague him, and see who'll get the best of it."

"Thank you, I guess I won't mind," responded Rob, in a dry

tone, which made the others laugh. He already knew by experience something of the pony's capers, though it had been in Leo's possession only a few weeks; while Jack, having been away on a visit, had never driven Winkie.

"Perhaps if you changed his name he would behave better," suggested Rob.

"I did think of that," answered Leo, seriously. "I had half a mind to call him Cream Puff; you see he's just the color of those lovely ones they sell at the baker's."

Both the boys laughed heartily.

"Crickey! that is an odd name, sure enough, and would suit him splendidly!" said Rob.

"Yes, and he'd have to be sweet and nice all the time, in order to live up to it," added Jack.

"Oh, you must not think he is ugly or vicious!" continued Leo. "He never tried to run away, and most of his antics are nothing but sport. He is not really bad, only a bit contrary occasionally, as Michael says. Mother declares that he reminds her sometimes of a boy who has forgotten to say his prayers in the morning, 'cause then he (the boy, you know) is apt to be fractious, and keeps getting into trouble all day."

"Ha, Leo, what a dead give away!" exclaimed Jack, in a badgering manner. "That's the way it is with you, is it?"

"That's the way with most fellows, I'll wager!" mumbled Leo, growing red, and wishing he had not been quite so communicative.

Neither of the others replied to this, but each secretly admitted that there was a good deal of truth in what he said.

They all assisted in harnessing Kittelywink, who appeared to think this great fun. However, when it became evident that he was expected to draw the little wagon laden with the lumber, he protested decidedly.

"He doesn't want to be used as a dray-horse," observed Leo, sympathetically.

Whether Winkie's pride was indeed hurt at being put to menial employment, or whether he simply felt it an imposition to require him to carry a pile of boards and three sturdy lads in addition, it is impossible to say. At all events, he refused to budge.

"Pshaw!" said Jack. "You fellows had better get off. I'll drive."

There was nothing to be done but for Rob and Leo to scramble down.

"Geet a-a-p!" cried Jack, giving the pony a sharp lash with the whip.

Winkle bounded forward, and darted up the road at what may be called literally a rattling speed; for the boards clattered away at every revolution of the wheels, and the driver found some difficulty in keeping his seat. Jack became excited. He sawed at the pony's mouth and drew him up so suddenly as to pull him back on his haunches. Winkie resolutely objected to these proceedings, and forthwith absolutely declined to go a step farther.

Rob and Leo came running up.

"Jingo, but he's a beauty!", exclaimed Rob, with admiring sincerity.

Winkie, in truth, looked very handsome and roguish as he stood there, with his head bent doggedly, his shaggy mane blown about by the wind, and his bright eyes mischievously asking as plainly as they could: "Well, what are you going to do about it?"

"Huh! Handsome is that handsome does!" grumbled Jack. "But I'll teach him to behave himself."

He raised the whip once more, but Leo caught his arm, crying,

"No, you must not whip him. Father says a horse can be managed by kindness better than in any other way."

"Oh, I *must* not!" repeated Jack, ironically; but, glancing at Leo's face, he saw that his cousin looked flushed and determined. It would not do to quarrel with such a little fellow as Leo, so he checked the sharp words that rose to his lips, and answered with an effort to be good-natured: "Try it yourself, then. I'll just sit here and hold the reins, and you can reason with him all you have a mind to."

Leo went up to the pony's head, patted and spoke gently to him. Winkie arched his neck, then put down his nose and coolly rubbed it all over his young master's face, as if deprecating his misconduct, while making his complaint, as it were, that he had not been fairly treated.

"If he isn't the cutest chap!" ejaculated Rob, delighted at his sagacity.

Jack could not help being amused also.

"Come now, Kittelywink, go 'long!" said he. "You shall have some sugar when I get home."

Most horses are very fond of sugar, and Winkie was no exception. He turned his ears back, with what Rob called "a pleased expression," at this propitiatory tone. But, although he enjoyed the petting now lavished upon him from all quarters, his sensibilities had apparently been too deeply wounded to admit of his being at once conciliated.

"I know!" suggested Jack, unwilling to relinquish the reins. "Suppose I ride on his back?"

Leo demurred till he saw that the pony did not oppose Jack's endeavor to mount. Winkie appeared to be under the impression that they were now to leave the wagon and the despised load behind. To the surprise of the boys he started ahead willingly, and Jack's spirits rose.

"Ha-ha! that's a good fellow!" he began.

Winkie went on a few rods. Presently he discovered that his expectations were not to be realized. The wagon was unusually heavy still; the clattering boards set up a racket every time he moved. He could not get away from them. It might be a good plan to try again, though. He capered and danced, then plunged onward. Jack did not look like a model horseman at this juncture. The boys screamed at him, giving contrary advice; though this made no difference, for his utmost exertions were directed to clinging to his refractory steed.

The pony was only annoyed, not frightened. He seemed to find Jack's efforts to keep from falling off quite entertaining. Suddenly a new idea occurred to him. What a wonder that he did not think of it before! He veered toward the side of the way, stopped abruptly, and, bending his head, sent Jack flying over it into the ditch. A grand success! With a satisfied air Winkie followed up his victory, approached his prostrate antagonist, regarded him for a moment, and - for he wore no check-line - putting down that clever nose of his, by a playful push with it he rolled the boy fairly over, and then set off in a steady trot along the highway.

II.

Winkie had just reached the gate of Jack's home, when our young friends caught up with him. Leo was now allowed to assume control, and, by dint of much coaxing and encouragement, at length succeeded in leading him to Mr. Gordon's barn. The wagon was here unloaded, after which Leo leaped into it, crying, "Come on, old fellow; that's all!" And Winkie, shaking his mane, as if felicitating himself that the disagreeable task was over, started off with much satisfaction.

"I'll be back again this afternoon," his little master shouted to the others as he drove away; "but - I think I'll walk!"

For the next fortnight the lads spent the greater part of the time in the Gordon barn. Such a hammering and sawing as went on there! At first the proceedings were enveloped in an air of mystery. Jack's father suspected that they were preparing for an amateur circus performance. His mother wondered at the interest manifested in the repair of the chicken-coops. Some experiment was in progress, she was sure; but what? At last the secret came out. They were building a boat!

Jack and Rob did it all. "The little boys" - as they were accustomed to call Jim and Leo, much to the chagrin of the latter - were not permitted to have anything to say. They were to keep their eyes open and learn by observation. This they did, though not with exactly the result that had been intended. Before long they understood very well what not to do in building a boat. But we are all liable to make mistakes; and are we not continually teaching others, at least by our experience?

In season and out of season the work went on. Little Barbara Stuart was constantly coming over to ask: "Is Rob here? Mother wants him; he hasn't half finished what he had to do at home." Leo kept getting into trouble because he would stop at his cousin's, instead of going directly home from school as his father wished him to do. Jim, who had a decided, but, alas! entirely uncultivated, taste for drawing, spoiled his new

MARY CATHERINE CROWLEY

writing-book with extraordinary sketches meant to represent every kind of boat, from a punt or dory to an ocean steamer; and in consequence was not on good terms with the school-master, who did not appreciate such evidences of genius.

Jack - well, everything seemed to go wrong with him. "Where is Jack?" - "Oh, bother, over at the barn!" The answer soon became a byword. The barn was at some distance from the house, and what a time there was in summoning the boy! The method was sufficiently telling, one would think, since it informed the whole neighborhood when he was wanted. It consisted in blowing the horn for him. Now, this was no common horn, but the voice of a giant imprisoned in a cylinder. Jack could have explained it upon the principle of compressed air, for he was studying natural philosophy; but Mr. Sheridan's Michael once described it in this way:

"Sure, it's the queerest thing that ever ye saw! Ye just jam one piece of tin pipe into another piece of tin pipe, as hard as ye can; an' it lets a wail out of it that ye'd think would strike terror to the heart of a stone and wake the dead!"

Whatever effect it might have upon granite or ghosts, however, Jack was usually so engrossed with the boat as to be deaf to its call. If Mrs. Gordon wanted him to harness a horse for her in a hurry, there was no use in sounding a bugle blast; she might try again and again, but in the end she would have to send some one over to him with the message. If he was sent up to the village on an errand, or told to do anything which took him away from his work, he either objected, or complied with a very bad grace.

"I'll tell ye one thing," said Mary Ann the cook, one day when neither Jack nor Jim would go to the store for her, though it would only have taken a few minutes to make the trip on the bicycle, - "I'll tell ye one thing, young sirs. Ye can't expect to have a bit of luck with that boat ye're buildin'."

"No luck! Why not, I'd like to know?" inquired Jack.

"Because all four of ye boys are neglectin' what ye ought to do, and takin' for this the time which by right should be spent on other things; because ye've given yer fathers and mothers more cause to find fault with ye durin' the last two or three weeks than for long before, all on account of it; because ye're none of ye so good-natured as ye used to be. I've heard that havin' a bee in the bonnet spoils a body; but faith I think a boat on the brain is worse. There's one thing, though, that my mind's made up to. I'll make no more cookies for young gentlemen that are not polite and obligin'."

Here was a threat! But, though the boys were secretly somewhat disconcerted, they would not give Mary Ann the satisfaction of seeing that either her prophecy or warning had any effect upon them.

"Pshaw, Mary Ann, you're so cross to-day!" declared Jim.

"It isn't always the good people who seem to have the best luck," continued Jack, braving it out. "And how can you tell whether we'll succeed or not? You are not a fortune-teller."

"Heaven forbid!" ejaculated Mary Ann, devoutly. "And, to be sure, there's plenty of people that gets on very successfully in the world, that don't seem to deserve to prosper half as much as others we know of. But God sees what we don't, and this much we may be certain of: wrong-doin' is always punished sooner or later; while we know that, in the end, those that tries to do right gets their full share of blessin's and a good bit over and above. I'm not sayin' indeed that ye won't build yer boat, only that if ye neglect yer duty ye'll have reason to regret it."

"Well, don't cast an 'evil eye' on the boat, anyway," said Jim; "for if we don't finish it, how can we ever give you a row on the creek?"

"Is it *I* ride in yer boat!" exclaimed Mary Ann, who was stout and short-breathed. The idea of trusting herself to the tender mercies of the lads, and venturing into any craft of their construction, was so ludicrous that she forgot her vexation and laughed heartily. "Faith, it's fine ballast I'd be for ye!" she said. "And is it in the middle of the river ye'd be landin' me? Thank ye kindly, but I'll not go a pleasurin' with ye. And as for an 'evil eye,' troth ye're but makin' game of my want of book-larnin'. But well I know there's no such thing; and if there was, it could never harm ye or yer work if ye were doin' right. So now be off with ye to the store, and bring me five pounds of sugar, quick as ye can. And if ye take the molasses jug along and get it filled - well, this once I'll beat up a batch of cookies, so ye can have some for yer lunch at school to-morrow."

III.

At last the wonderful boat was pronounced finished. It had obviously not been modeled with an eye to beauty - was flat as the barn floor, square at both ends, and entirely lacking in the curves which constitute the grace of the seabird-like craft which are the delight of yachtmen. Nevertheless, the boys were proud of it. It was their own: they had built it themselves.

"There she is, complete from bow to stern!" exclaimed Jack, with a satisfied air.

"Yes," responded Leo, admiringly. "But" - hesitating - "but - which is the bow and which the stern, you know - eh?"

"Why, this end, stupid! Don't you see I've marked it with a cross?" answered Jack.

"Perhaps I *am* stupid," thought Leo; "for I don't understand now how one end can be both. I wish Jack would be a little more particular about explaining a thing. It's queer how few fellows are! They jumble their words all up, and think that because *they* know what they mean, you ought to understand, of course."

"Well," observed Jim, quizzically, "she isn't quite as handsome as the barges on the lake in the park, that float up and down, looking like white swans. Yes, I guess she'll do."

"We didn't set out to build a gondola, to paddle children and nursery maids around in," retorted Rob, with a withering glance. "She's a good, serviceable boat, and safe - "

"Oh, safe as a tub!" agreed Jim, hastily, intending the remark as conciliatory.

"Huh! Perhaps you never tried to pilot a tub," interposed Leo. "I did the other day, just for practice, so I'd know how to row when the time came to use this here punt - if that's what you call it. Jimminy! I got tipped over into the creek, and a scolding besides when I went home! I'd be sorry to have her act like that."

"A tub is a tub and a boat is a boat," said Jack, sententiously. "This one couldn't tip over if it tried. Don't you see it's most square? In fact, we didn't mean to get it quite so wide; but, after all, it is better than those canoe-like things, which are always rocking from one side to the other."

"What are you going to name it?" asked Jim.

Jack looked nonplussed. This necessity had not occurred to him before. He appealed to Rob.

"Suppose," replied the latter, after mature deliberation, - "suppose we call it the Sylph? There's a, story in the *Boys' Own* about a beautiful boat called the Sylph."

"Cricky! it looks about as much like a sylph as - well, as Mary Ann does!" said Jim. Since the stout, good-natured cook was heavy, and nearly square in figure, the comparison was amusingly apt.

"Do you remember the tents at Coney Island in summer, where a regular wooden circus procession goes round in a ring, keeping time to the music?" asked Leo.

"Yes, and by paying five cents you can take your choice, and ride on a zebra or a lion or a big gold ostrich, or anything that's there. And once we chose a *scrumptious* boat, all blue and silver, and drawn by two swans," responded Jim.

"Well, what was the name of that?" said Leo.

"I think the man told us she was known as the *Fairy*," answered Jim.

Again they looked at the boat and shook their heads. It would not do.

"I did not mean the name of the blue and silver barge, but of the whole thing - the ring and all?" added Leo.

"Oh, the *Merry-go-Round*," said Jack.

"Why would not that be a good name?" argued Rob, pleased with the sound, and, like many a person whose fancy is caught by the jingle of a word, paying little attention to its sense.

"That is what I thought," began Leo, delighted to find his motion seconded, as he would have explained in the language of the juvenile debating society, which met periodically in that very barn.

"Why! do you expect this boat to keep going round and round when we get it out into the middle of the creek?" said practical Jack, pretending to be highly indignant at the imputation.

"No indeed," disclaimed Rob. "Only that she would go around everywhere - up and down the stream, you know; and on an exploring expedition, as we proposed."

"That is not so bad," Jack admitted. "Still, I think we could get a better name. Let us see! The Merry Sailor, - how's that?"

"N - no - hardly," murmured Bob.

"The Jolly Sail - I have it: the Jolly Pioneer!"

"Hurrah!" cried Jim. "The very thing!"

"Yes, I guess that fits pretty well," acknowledged Rob.

"It's capital!" volunteered Leo.

And so the matter was finally settled. The *Jolly Pioneer* was still destitute of paint, but the boys were in so great a hurry to launch her that they decided not to delay on this account. They carried her down to the creek, and by means of a board slid her into the water. Jack got into the boat first, while the others held the side close to the bank. After him came Rob. Jim and Leo were to follow, but the *Jolly Pioneer* seemed to have dwindled in size, and did not look half so big or imposing as when in the barn.

"Hold on!" cried Jack. "I'm afraid you will be too heavy. It won't do to crowd at first. We'll just row gently with the current a short distance, and then come back and let you have a turn."

Though disappointed, the little fellows did not demur, but handed him the oars, and waited to see the two boys glide away. But, alas! though the *Jolly Pioneer* moved a little, it was not with the freedom and confidence which was to be expected of her in her native element. She seemed to shrink and falter, "as if afraid of getting wet," as Jim laughingly declared.

"Hello! what's that?" exclaimed Rob, as he felt something cold at his feet. He looked down: his shoes were thoroughly wet; the water was coming in through the crevices of the boat.

"Pshaw!" cried Jack. "That is because it is new yet; when the wood is soaked it will swell a bit. Hurry and bail out the water, though."

"But we haven't anything to do it with," returned Rob, helplessly.

"Oh, take your hat, man! A fine sailor you'd make!" Jack answered, setting the example by dipping in his own old felt. Rob's was a new straw yet. Unfortunately for its appearance during the remainder of the summer, he did not think of this, but immediately went to work. Their efforts were of no use: the *Jolly Pioneer* sank slowly but surely.

"Don't give up the ship!" cried Jack, melodramatically.

So as neither of the boys attempted to get out, and thus lessen the weight, down, down it went, till it reached the pebbly bed of the creek, and they found themselves - still in the boat to be sure, but standing up to their waists in water. The worst of the mortification was that the little fellows, high and dry on the bank, were choking with laughter, which finally could no longer be suppressed, and broke forth in a merry peal.

"What do you want to stand there guffawing for?" called Jack, ill-naturedly. "Why don't you try to get the oars?"

Thus made to realize that they might be of some assistance, Jim and Leo waded in heroically, unmindful of the effect upon shoes, stockings, and clothing generally, and rescued the oars, of which poor Jack had carelessly relaxed his hold in the effort to bail out the boat, and which were being carried swiftly away by the current.

In the meantime Jack and Rob succeeded in raising the *Jolly Pioneer* and hauling her up on the bank. While they stood there, contemplating her in discouragement, and regardless of their own bedraggled condition, who should come along but Uncle Gerald.

"Hie! what is the matter?" he called from the road, suspecting the situation at once.

"Something is wrong with the blamed boat, after all!" Jack shouted back, impatiently.

Uncle Gerald leaped over the low wall, which separated the highway from the meadow, and was presently among them, surveying the unfortunate *Pioneer*, which now did not look at all jolly, but wore a dejected appearance, one might fancy, as if out of conceit with itself at having proved such a miserable failure.

"There! I suppose he'll say, 'If you had not been so positive that you knew all about boatbuilding - if you had come to me

MARY CATHERINE CROWLEY

for the advice I promised you, - this would not have happened,'" thought Jack; feeling that (like the story of the last straw placed upon the overladen pack-horse, which proved too much for its strength) to be thus reminded would make the burden of his vexations greater than he could bear.

Uncle Gerald might indeed have moralized in some such fashion, but he considerately refrained, and only remarked, kindly:

"Do not be disheartened. This is not such bad work for a first attempt. The boat would look better if it were painted, and that would fill up a few of the cracks too. As some of the boards are not dovetailed together, you should have calked the seams with oakum."

"To be sure!" responded Jack. "How could we have had so little gumption as not to have thought of it?"

"Oakum is hemp obtained from untwisting old ropes," continued Uncle Gerald. "In genuine ship-building, calking consists in crowding threads of this material with great force into the seams between the planks. When filled, they are then rubbed over with pitch, or what is known as marine glue, - a composition of shellac and caoutchouc. It will not be necessary for you to do all this, however. Oakum is often used for packing goods also. I dare say if you hunt around in the barn you will find a little lying about somewhere. But, bless me, you young rogues! Here you are all this time in your wet clothes. Leo, your mother will be worried for fear you may take cold. Run home as fast as you can and get into a dry suit. And you other fellows, come! We'll take the *Jolly Pioneer* back to the workshop without delay; and then you must hurry and do the same."

IV.

Many days had not passed before the boys succeeded in making the punt water-tight. Yet the carpentering still went on at the barn.

"What is all the hammering for now?" asked Mr. Gordon one afternoon. "I thought the *Jolly Pioneer* was in splendid trim and doing good service."

"So she is," answered Jack. "But - well, she doesn't quite come up to our expectations; so Rob and I have given her to the little boys. We are building a larger boat for ourselves."

Upon the principle "Never look a gift-horse in the mouth," Jim and Leo were not disposed to find anything amiss with the present. In the first flush of their pride of possession they were quite jubilant.

It was shortly after this that Jim came in to dinner one day, tattooed in a manner which would remind one of a sachem in full Indian war-paint. There was a patch of blue low down on one cheek, a daub of red high up on the other, a tip of chrome-yellow on the end of his nose, and a fair share of all three upon his hands, and the sleeve of his jacket as well.

"Why, my son!" exclaimed Mrs. Gordon, as this vision met her eyes.

"Can't help it, mother, - it won't come off. I've scrubbed and scrubbed!" the little fellow protested, apologetically.

"Plenty of hot water and soap will prove effectual. But you must persevere," she went on, good-naturedly. "But what is the reason of this extraordinary decoration? Do you want to be taken for the 'missing link'?"

Mrs. Gordon was always good friends with her boys. She had a bright, cheery way of talking to them, of entering into their plans. She thoroughly appreciated a joke, even a practical one, when it was not perpetrated at the expense of anybody's feelings. And the lads could always count upon her interest and sympathy. It was not easy to impose upon her, though. "I tell you, if a fellow tries, he is always sure to get the worst of it!" Jim used to say.

"Ah, that is better!" said she, when Jim returned to the dining-room, his face at last restored to its usual sunburnt hue, and shining from the effect of a liberal lather of soap-suds, and his hands also of a comparatively respectable color. "Now, do tell us what you have been attempting."

"Haven't been attempting anything," he mumbled. "Leo and I were painting our boat, that is all. We hurried so as to finish it before dinner. I suppose that is the reason the paint got splashed around a little."

Jim's temper had manifestly been somewhat ruffled by the necessity of repeating the soap and water process. He frowned like a thundercloud.

Mrs. Gordon, however, always had great consideration for a hungry boy. Without appearing to notice that Jim was out of sorts, she merely remarked, while helping him bountifully to beefsteak: "You have painted the *Jolly Pioneer*? How well she must look! I believe I'll walk over to the barn after dinner and see her."

"Will you really, mother?" he exclaimed, brightening at once.

"Yes, certainly. What color did you choose?"

"Blue, with red and yellow trimmings," answered the boy, exultingly.

His mother smiled. She had inferred so. But Jim's ill-humor had vanished like mists before the sun. The next moment he was explaining to her the merits of various kinds of paint, and discussing the question with Jack, in the best possible spirits.

V.

Jack and Rob took counsel with Mr. Sheridan in the construction of the new boat, and very creditable and satisfactory was the result. The ceremonies of the launch were now to be observed with as much formality as if she were the crack yacht of the season, - "Barrin' the traditional bottle of champagne, which it is customary to break over the bows of the new skiff as she plunges into the sea," laughed Uncle Gerald; "and that would not do at all for you, boys."

"No, sir," answered Jack, decidedly. "If it was as cheap and as plentiful as soda-water, we wouldn't have it."

"I am glad to hear you say that," continued Leo's father, warmly. "It is one of the best resolutions to start in life with."

"You know, we have joined the temperance cadet corps which Father Martin is getting up," explained Rob.

"An excellent plan. I had not heard of it," responded the gentleman. "Persevere, and you will find that by encouraging you in this, Father Martin has proved one of the truest friends you are ever likely to have. However, the old custom of christening a boat, as it is called, may be carried out quite as effectively with a bottle of ginger-pop, which Leo has stowed away somewhere in that basket. It is the part of common-sense to unite true poetry and prose, just as we now propose to combine a picturesque custom with temperance principles. So, boys, hurrah for ginger-pop, say I!"

The lads entered into the spirit of his mood with great gusto, and cheered hilariously. The basket was produced, and at this moment Mrs. Gordon was seen coming across the meadow. "Just in time, mother!" cried Jack, starting off to meet her.

"You must christen the boat!" vociferated all.

"And is that the reason why Uncle Gerald sent for me, and

brought me away from my morning's mending?" she exclaimed, in a tone which was intended to be slightly reproachful, though she looked prepared for anything that might be required of her; for Mrs. Gordon, somehow, managed never to be so busy as to be unable to enter into the pleasures of her boys.

"Yes," acknowledged Uncle Gerald; "and I have been doing my utmost to delay the proceedings, so that you would not miss them. You see, Leo and I have prepared a little surprise for the company."

After a comprehensive glance at the basket, which certainly appeared well packed, she asked:

"And what is to be the name of the boat?"

"We have not quite decided yet, Mrs. Gordon," began Rob.

"No," interposed Jack. "We think *this* ought to be the *Jolly Pioneer*. We let Jim and Leo have the other boat, but we didn't mean to give them the name too. We chose it, and we can't think of any we like so well."

"Oh, keep it, then!" answered Jim, with a wave of the hand like that of a stage hero resigning a fortune. (It was evident that the subject had been broached before.) "We are quite able to choose a name ourselves; we could think of half a dozen others if we wanted to, so you are welcome to call your boat whatever you please."

The permission might, indeed, have been more graciously expressed; but as Jim's words were accompanied by a good-natured smile. Jack wondered if he might not accept it.

Mrs. Gordon stood, with the bottle in her hand, waiting for the decision, but wisely refraining from comment; the boys always settled their little disputes for themselves.

MARY CATHERINE CROWLEY

"Well, what shall it be? Speak!" she said.

"The *Jolly Pioneer!*" cried both.

The next moment there was a crash of broken glass and a dash of ginger-pop on what was called by courtesy the bow.

"Bravo! The Jolly Pioneer is a new recruit enlisted into the temperance cadet corps," said Uncle Gerald, laughing.

There was a shifting of planks by Rob and Jack, and in another moment the little craft was dancing gaily upon the bright waters.

"Hurrah, hurrah!" cried the boys in chorus.

By turns they rowed a short distance down the stream and back. There was no danger of sinking this time. Then they gathered under the tree, where Mrs. Gordon and Uncle Gerald had unpacked the basket and set forth a tempting lunch upon a tablecloth on the grass. As hunger is said to be the best sauce, so good-humor sweetens the simplest fare. Our friends enjoyed their sandwiches and doughnuts, and milk rich with cream, as much as if a banquet had been spread before them. There was plenty of fun, too; and though the wit was not very brilliant, it was innocent and kindly, and served its purpose; for the company were quite ready to be pleased at any one's effort to be entertaining or amusing.

After an hour or more, Mrs. Gordon announced her intention of returning to the house.

"And I must be off also; for I have to drive two or three miles up country, about some business," added her brother.

"We shall all have to leave now," said Jack. "Father Martin is going to drill the cadets for a short time in the early part of the afternoon."

"What arrangements have you made for fastening your boat?" asked Uncle Gerald. "To guard against its being tampered with by meddlesome persons, as well as to prevent its drifting away, you ought to secure it to a stake near the bank by means of a padlock."

"We forgot to get one," returned Jack. "No one will touch it here. I'll tie it to a tree with this piece of rope, so that it won't go floating off on an exploring expedition on its own account."

The next day was Sunday, and the boys had no chance to use the boat again until Monday after school. When they hurried to the spot where it had been moored, alas! the *Jolly Pioneer* was nowhere to be seen.

"Do you think she broke away?" asked Leo.

"Pshaw! The *Jolly Pioneer* isn't a pony!" impatiently answered Jack.

"But the rope might have snapped," said Jim.

"No: the boat has been stolen," muttered Bob, gloomily.

"I don't believe that," continued Jim. "Perhaps some of the fellows around have hidden her, just to plague us."

"I bet it was those Jenkins boys!" declared Jack. "Don't you remember, Rob, how we made them stop badgering little Tommy Casey in the school-yard the other day, and how mad they were about it?"

"Yes, and they swore they'd be even with us," answered Rob.

The Jenkins boys were the children of a drunken father, a slatternly mother. Brought up in a comfortless, poverty-stricken home, without any religious teaching or influences, what wonder that they became addicted to most of the petty vices, - that they acquired an unenviable reputation for

MARY CATHERINE CROWLEY

mischief, mendacity, and thieving in a small way?

Jack's inference could hardly be called a rash judgment. A glimpse of a derisive, grinning face among the neighboring bushes confirmed his suspicions. Without a word he made a dash toward the thicket. His companions understood, however, and were not slow to follow his example. There was a crackling of the brambles, succeeded by a stampede. Jack, with all his alertness, had not been quite quick enough. With a jeering whoop, two shabby figures escaped into the road.

"The question is, where's the boat?" said Rob, as the party paused for breath, finding that pursuit was useless.

They searched about in the vicinity without avail, but after some time the *Jolly Pioneer* was finally discovered half a mile farther down the stream, entangled among a clump of willows, where the pirates, as Jim designated the Jenkins boys, had abandoned it. To return to the place from which they had taken the boat, in order to enjoy the discomfiture and dismay of those against whom they had a grudge, was characteristic of them.

"Good! I knew we'd find the boat all right!" began Leo, joyfully.

"By Jove! pretty well damaged, I should say!" cried Jack.

"Well, the paint is a good deal scratched, and the seats have been loosened; but, after all, there is no great harm done," said Rob, more hopefully.

Upon further examination, his view of the case proved to be correct. He and Jack experienced but little difficulty in rowing back to the original moorings, Jim and Leo following along the bank and applauding their skill.

After this occurrence the *Jolly Pioneer* and the *Merry-go-Round* were each fastened to a sapling, that grew near the water's edge, by chain and padlock, which rendered them secure from interference.

And what merry times our friends had with them upon the creek that summer! The *Jolly Pioneer* proved worthy of its name, was always the best of company, and led the way in many pleasant excursions up and down the stream. The *Merry-go-Round* was never far behind, and shared the honors of all its adventures.

"I tell you now," exclaimed Leo, admiringly, one day when the lads were preparing for a row, "I don't believe you'd find two such boats in all the country about here."

A critical observer might have facetiously agreed with him, but the boys were content with what they had, not being able to obtain anything better; and is not that one way to be happy?

"Well, they may not be beauties," continued Jim; "and you can't exactly call them racers; but, somehow, they keep afloat, and one can manage them first-rate."

"And we've had enough fun with them to repay us for all the trouble we had in making them," added Rob.

Jack laughed at the recollection.

"Yes," remarked Uncle Gerald, who had just come up, on his way to the meadow pasture. "And I think, boys, you will all acknowledge that you learned a good many useful things while building a boat."

A MAY-DAY GIFT

I.

Early on the morning of the 1st of May, Abby Clayton ran downstairs, exclaiming by way of greeting to the household:

"A bright May Day! A bright May Day!"

"It isn't very *bright*, I'm sure!" grumbled her little brother Larry, who clattered after her. "There's no sunshine; and the wind blows so hard I sha'n't be able to sail my new boat on the pond in the park. It's mighty hard lines! I don't see why it can't be pleasant on a holiday. Think of all the shiny days we've had when a fellow had to be in school. Now, when there's a chance for some fun, it looks as if it were going to rain great guns!"

"Well, it won't," said Abby, pausing in the hall to glance back at him, as he perched upon the baluster above her. "It won't rain great guns, nor pitchforks, nor cats and dogs, nor even torrents. It's going to clear up. Don't you know that some people say the sun generally shines, for a few minutes anyhow, on Saturdays in honor of the Blessed Virgin?"

"This isn't Saturday," objected Larry, somewhat indignantly.

"Yes, but it is the 1st of May; and if that is not our Blessed Mother's day too, I'd like to know what is!" said his sister.

"I don't believe that about the sun shining," continued Larry. "If you are ten - only two years older than I am, - you don't know everything. I'm going to ask mother."

The children entered the breakfast room, greeted their father and mother, and then slipped into their places.

"Mother," began Larry, as he slowly poured the maple syrup over the crisp, hot pancakes upon his plate, "is it true that the sun always shines on Saturday in honor of the Blessed Virgin?"

"It is a pious and poetic saying," replied Mrs. Clayton. "But a legendary sentiment of this kind often hides a deeper meaning. For those who are devoted to the Blessed Virgin, there is never a day so dark but that the love of Our Lady shines through the gloom like a sunbeam, changing to the rosy and golden tints of hope the leaden clouds that shadowed their happiness; and blessing the closing day of life, which, to look back upon, seems but as the ending of a week."

Mrs. Clayton had hardly finished speaking, when a long ray of yellow light fell upon the tablecloth.

"There! the sun's out now, anyway! Crickey, I'm so glad!" exclaimed Larry.

"The clouds were only blown up by the wind," said his father. "I do not think we shall have rain to-day."

"Mother, may I put on a white dress and go to buy my May wreath?" asked Abby.

"The air is too cold for you to change your warm gown for a summer one, dear," returned Mrs. Clayton. "You may get the wreath, though; but be sure that you wear it over your hat."

Abby seemed to think it was now her turn to grumble.

"Oh, dear!" she murmured. "All the girls wear white dresses, and go without hats on May Day. I don't see why I can't!"

Her complaint made no impression, however; so she flounced out of the room.

"My mother is the most exaggerating person!" exclaimed the little girl, as she prepared for her shopping excursion. She meant aggravating; but, like most people who attempt to use large words the meaning of which they do not understand, she made droll mistakes sometimes.

Abby had fifteen cents, which her grandma had given her the day before.

"I'll hurry down to the Little Women's before the best wreaths are gone," she said to herself.

The place was a fancy store, kept by two prim but pleasant spinster sisters. Besides newspapers, stationery, thread and needles, and so forth, they kept a stock of toys, candies, and pickled limes, which insured them a run of custom among the young folk, who always spoke of them as the Little Women. Not to disappoint the confidence placed in them by their youthful patrons, they had secured an excellent assortment of the crowns of tissue-paper flowers which, in those days, every little girl considered essential to the proper observance of May Day.

Abby selected one which she and the Little Women made up their minds was the prettiest. It usually took both of the Little Women to sell a thing. If one showed it, the other descanted upon its merits, or wrapped it up in paper when the bargain was completed. Neither of them appeared to transact any business, even to the disposal of "a pickle lime" (as the children say), quite on her own responsibility.

After Abby had fully discussed the matter with them, therefore, she bought her wreath. It was made of handsome white tissue-paper roses, with green tissue-paper leaves, and had two long streamers. There was another of pink roses, which she thought would be just the thing for Larry to buy with the fifteen cents which he had received also. But Larry had said:

"Pshaw! I wouldn't wear a wreath!" Abby didn't see why, because some boys wore them.

On the way home she met a number of her playmates. Several of them shivered in white dresses, and all were bareheaded except for their paper wreaths. Not one of the wreaths was so fine as Abby's, however. But, then, few little girls had fifteen cents to expend upon one. Abby perceived at a glance that most of those worn by her companions were of the ten-cent variety. The Little Women had them for eight; and even five copper pennies would buy a very good one, although the roses of the five-cent kind were pronounced by those most interested to be "little bits of things."

Abby talked to the girls a while, and then went home to exhibit her purchase. Her mother commented approvingly upon it; and the little girl ran down to the kitchen to show it to Delia the cook, who had lived with the family ever since Larry was a baby.

Delia was loud in her admiration.

"Oh, on this day they do have great doings in Ireland!" said she; "but nowadays, to be sure, it's nothing to what it was in old times. It was on May eve, I've heard tell, that St. Patrick lit the holy fire at Tara, in spite of the ancient pagan laws. And in the days when the country was known as the island of saints and of scholars, sure throughout the length and breadth of the land the monastery bells rang in the May with praises of the Holy Mother; and the canticles in her honor were as ceaseless as the song of the birds. And 'twas the fairies that were said to have great power at this season -"

"Delia, you know very well there are no fairies," interrupted Abby.

"Well, some foolish folk thought there were, anyhow,"

answered Delia. "And in Maytide the children and cattle, the milk and the butter, were kept guarded from them. Many and many an evening I've listened to my mother that's dead and gone - God rest her soul! - telling of an old woman that, at the time of the blooming of the hawthorn, always put a spent coal under the churn, and another beneath the grandchild's cradle, because that was said to drive the fairies away; and how primroses used to be scattered at the door of the house to prevent the fairies from stealing in, because they could not pass that flower. But you don't hear much of that any more; for the priest said 'twas superstition, and down from the heathenish times. So the old people came to see 'twas wrong to use such charms, and the young people laughed at the old women's tales. Now on May Day the shrines in the churches are bright with flowers, of course. And as for the innocent merrymakings, instead of a dance round the May or hawthorn bush, as in the olden times, in some places there's just perhaps a frolic on the village green, when the boys and girls come home from the hills and dales with their garlands of spring blossoms - not paper flowers like those," added Delia, with a contemptuous glance at Abby's wreath, forgetting how much she had admired it only a few moments before.

Somehow it did not now seem so beautiful to Abby either. She took it off, and gazed at it with a sigh.

"Here in New England the boys and girls go a-Maying," she said. "Last year, when we were in the country, Larry and I went with our cousins. We had such fun hanging May-baskets! I got nine. But," she went on, regretfully, "I don't expect any this year; for city children do not have those plays."

She went upstairs to the sitting-room, where Larry was rigging his boat anew. He had been to the pond, but the wind wrought such havoc with the little craft that he had to put into port for repairs.

Half an hour passed. Abby was dressing her beloved doll for an airing on the sidewalk, - a promenade in a carriage, as the

French say. While thus occupied she half hummed, half sang, in a low voice, to herself, a popular May hymn. When she reached the refrain, Larry joined, and Delia appeared at the door just in time to swell the chorus with honest fervor:

"See, sweet Mary, on thy altars
Bloom the fairest flowers of May.
Oh, may we, earth's sons and daughters,
Grow by grace as fair as they!"

"If you please," said Delia at its close, "there's a man below stairs who says he has something for you both."

"For us!" exclaimed the children, starting up.

"Yes: your mother sent me to tell you. He says he was told to say as how he had a May-basket for you."

"A May-basket, Delia? What! All lovely flowers like those I told you about?" cried the little girl.

"Sure, child, and how could I see what was inside, and it so carefully done up?" answered Delia, evasively.

They did not question further, but rushed downstairs to see for themselves.

In the kitchen waited a foreign-looking man, with swarthy skin, and thin gold rings in his ears. On the floor beside him was a large, rough packing-basket.

"*That* a May-basket!" exclaimed Abby, hardly able to restrain the tears of disappointment which started to her eyes.

"*Si, signorita,*" replied the man.

Her frown disappeared. It was certainly very nice to be addressed by so high-sounding a title. She wished she could get Delia to call her *signorita*. But no; she felt sure that Delia never would.

"Pshaw! It's only a joke!" said Larry, after a moment. "Somebody thinks this is April-fool Day, I guess."

"Have patience for a leetle minute, please," said the man, as he cast away the packing bit by bit. The children watched him with eager interest. By and by he took out a little bunch of lilies of the valley, which he handed to Abby with a low bow. Next he came to something shrouded in fold after fold of tissue-paper.

"And here is the fairest lily of them all," he said, in his poetic Italian fashion.

"What can it be, mother?" asked the little girl, wonderingly.

Mrs. Clayton smiled. "It is from Sartoris', the fine art store where you saw the beautiful pictures last week; that is all I know about it," she replied.

The man carefully placed the mysterious object on the table.

"It is some kind of a vase or an image," declared Larry.

"Why, so it is!" echoed Abby.

In another moment the tissue veil was torn aside, and there stood revealed a beautiful statue of the Blessed Virgin.

"Oh!" exclaimed Larry, in delight.

"How lovely!" added his sister.

The image was about two feet high, and of spotless Parian, which well symbolized the angelic purity it was intended to portray. To many, perhaps, it might appear simply a specimen of modeling, but little better than the average. However, those who looked on it with the eyes of faith saw before them, not so much the work itself, as the ideal of the artist.

The graceful figure or Our Lady at once suggested the ethereal and celestial. The long mantle, which fell in folds to her feet, signified her modesty and motherly protection; the meekly folded hands were a silent exhortation to humility and prayer; the tender, spiritual face invited confidence and love; the crown upon her brow proclaimed her sovereignty above all creatures and her incomparable dignity as Mother of God.

"And is this beautiful statue really ours - just Larry's and mine?" asked Abby.

"So the messenger says," returned Mrs. Clayton.

"Who could have sent it, I wonder?" inquired Larry.

The Italian pointed to the card attached to the basket. Abby took it off and read:

> "To my little friends, Abby and Larry Clayton, with the hope that, especially during this month, they will try every day to do some little thing to honor our Blessed Mother.
>
> "FATHER DOMINIC."

"From Father Dominic!" exclaimed the boy, in delight.

"How very good of him!" added Abby, gratefully.

Father Dominic - generally so called because his musical Italian surname was a stumbling-block to our unwieldy English speech - was a particular friend of Mr. and Mrs. Clayton, who appreciated his culture and refinement, and admired his noble character and devotion to his priestly duties. He was an occasional visitor at their house, and took a great interest in the children.

"How nice of him to send us something we shall always have!"

Abby ran on. "Now I can give the tiny image in my room to some one who hasn't any."

"May we make an altar for our statue, mother?" asked Larry.

Although as a rule a lively, rollicking boy, when it came to anything connected with his prayers, he was unaffectedly and almost comically solemn about it.

"Yes," responded Mrs. Clayton. "And I think it would be a good plan also to frame the card and hang it on the front of the altar, so that you may not forget Father Dominic's words: 'Try every day to do some little thing to honor our Blessed Mother.'"

II.

"O mother!" cried Abby, the day after the arrival of the unique May-basket from Father Dominic, "now that we have such a lovely statue of the Blessed Virgin, don't you think we ought to make a regular altary."

"A what!" exclaimed Mrs. Clayton, at a loss to understand what her little daughter could possibly mean. "I told you that you might have an altar, dear. And you may arrange it when-ever you please."

"No, but an altary," persisted Abby. "The Tyrrells have an altary in their house, and I wish we could have one too. Why, you must know what it is, mother, - just a little room fitted up like a chapel; and the family say their prayers there night and morning, and at other times if they wish."

"Oh, an oratory!" observed Mrs. Clayton, trying to repress a smile.

"Perhaps that *is* the name," admitted Abby, a trifle disconcerted. "Anyhow, can't we have one?"

"Well - yes," said her mother, after a few moments' reflection. "The small room next to the parlor might be arranged for that purpose."

"That would make a beautiful al - chapel!" exclaimed Abby. She did not venture to attempt the long word again.

"I think I could get enough out of the carpet that was formerly on the parlor to cover the floor," mused Mrs. Clayton aloud. "The square table, draped with muslin and lace, would make a pretty altar. Then, with the pictures of the Sacred Heart and the Bouguereau Madonna to hang on the walls, and my *prie-dieu* - yes, Abby, I think we can manage it."

"Oh, how splendid!" cried the little girl. "When shall we begin to get it ready?"

"Perhaps to-morrow," answered her mother; "but I can not promise to have the preparations completed at once. It will take some time to plan the carpet and have it put down."

Abby was not only satisfied, but delighted. She told Larry the minute he came into the house. He had been over to the pond with his boat again.

"That will be grand!" said he. "When you get everything fixed, I'll bring you the little vase I got for Christmas, and my prayer-book, and - oh, yes, my rosary, to put on the altar. And, then," he went on, quite seriously, "there's my catechism, and the little chalk angel, and -"

"The little chalk angel!" repeated Abby, scornfully. "Why, that has lost its head!"

"But it's a little chalk angel all the same," argued Larry. "And if I find the head, it can be glued on."

"Oh - well; we don't want any trash like that on our altar!" rejoined his sister. "And the books and rosary can be kept on the shelf in the corner. It would be nice to have the vase, though."

Larry, who at first had been rather offended that his offerings were not appreciated, brightened up when he found he could at least furnish something to adorn the shrine.

The following day was Saturday. There was, of course, no school, and Abby was free to help her mother to get the little room in order. She was impatient to begin. But alas for her plans! About nine o'clock in the morning Mrs. Clayton suddenly received word that grandma was not feeling well, and she at once prepared to visit the dear old lady.

"I may be away the greater part of the day, Delia," she said, as she tied the strings of her bonnet; "but I have given you all necessary directions, I think, - Larry, do not go off with any of the boys, but you may play in the park as usual. - And, Abby, be sure that you do not keep Miss Remick waiting when she comes to give you your music lesson."

"But what about the altary - oh, oratory I mean?" asked Abby, dejectedly.

"There is a piece of muslin in the linen press which you may take to cover the altar," said her mother; "but do not attempt to arrange anything more. I will attend to the rest next week. I am sorry to disappoint you and Larry; but, you see, I can not help it."

She harried away; and the children ran up to the parlor, which was on the second story of the house, to take another look at their precious statue, which had been placed on the marble slab in front of one of the long mirrors. Then they went into the small room which was to be the oratory. The only furniture it contained was the square table which they had brought there the evening before. Abby got the muslin, and began to drape the table to resemble an altar; Larry looking on admiringly, volunteering a suggestion now and then. She succeeded pretty well. Larry praised her efforts; he was prouder than ever of his sister, - although, as he remarked, "the corners *would* look a little bunchy, and the cloth was put on just a *teenty* bit crooked."

Presently the little girl paused, took several pins out of her mouth - which seemed to be the most available pincushion, - and glanced disconsolately at the pine boards of the floor.

"What is the use of fixing the altar before the floor is covered!" she said. "I am almost sure I could put down the carpet myself."

"Oh, no, you couldn't!" said Larry. "You'd be sure to hammer your fingers instead of the tacks - girls always do. But if you

MARY CATHERINE CROWLEY

get the carpet all spread out, *I'll* nail it down for you."

The roll of carpet stood in the corner. It had been partially ripped apart, and there were yards and yards of it; for it had covered the parlor, which was a large room. Mrs. Clayton intended to have it made over for the dining-room, and estimated that there would be enough left for the oratory. She had not thought it necessary to explain these details to Abby, however.

"We'll do it," declared the latter. "Mother said to wait, but I don't believe she'll care."

"Course she won't," agreed Larry.

Both the children felt that what they had decided upon was not exactly right, - that it would be better to observe strictly their mother's instructions. But, like many people who argue themselves into the delusion that what they want to do is the best thing to be done, Abby tried to compromise with the "still small voice" which warned her not to meddle, by the retort: "Oh, it will spare mother the trouble! And she'll be glad to have it finished." As for Larry, the opportunity to pound away with the hammer and make as much noise as he pleased, was a temptation hard to resist.

Abby opened the roll.

"What did mother mean by saying she thought she could get enough out of this carpet to cover the floor?" said the little girl, with a laugh. "She must have been very absent-minded; for there's lashin's of it here, as Delia would say."

"Oh, my, yes - lashin's!" echoed Larry.

Abby was what is called "a go-ahead" young person. She was domestic in her tastes, and, for her years, could make herself very useful about the house when she chose. Now, therefore, she had no diffidence about her ability to carry out her undertaking. And Larry, although he frequently reminded her that she did not know *every*thing, had a flattering confidence in her capacity.

"I'll have it done in less than no time," she said, running to get her mother's large scissors.

Click, click went the shears as she slashed into the carpet, taking off breadth after breadth, without attempting to match the pattern, and with little regard for accuracy of measurement. Instead of laying it along the length of the room, she chose to put it crosswise, thus cutting it up into any number of short pieces.

"No matter about its not being sewed," she went on; "you can nail it together, can't you, Larry?"

"Oh, yes!" said Larry.

The more hammering the better for him. He hunted up the hammer and two papers of tacks, and as fast as Abby cut he nailed.

Delia was unusually busy; for it was house-cleaning time, and she was getting the diningroom ready for the new carpet. Therefore, although she heard the noise upstairs, she gave herself no concern about it; supposing that Larry was merely amusing himself, for he was continually tinkering at one thing or another.

By and by Larry remarked: "Say, Abby, you've got two of these pieces too short."

Abby went over and looked at them. "Gracious, so I have!" she said. "Well, put them aside, and I'll cut two more."

Click went the scissors again, and the carpet was still further mutilated. Then, as a narrow strip was required, a breadth was slit down the centre. Finally the boards were covered.

"There!" she cried triumphantly. "It is all planned. Now, I'll nail."

Larry demurred at first, but Abby was imperious. Moreover, the constant friction of the handle of the hammer had raised a blister in the palm of his hand. Abby had an ugly red welt around her thumb, caused by the resistance of the scissors; for it had been very hard work to cut the heavy carpet. But she did not complain, for she felt that she was a martyr to industry.

At last the work was completed; and, flushed and tired, with her fingers bruised from frequent miscalculated blows from the hammer, and her knuckles rubbed and tingling, she paused to admire the result of her toil. The carpeting was a curious piece of patchwork certainly, but the children were delighted with their achievement.

The lunch bell rang.

"Don't say anything about it to Delia," cautioned Abby.

Larry agreed that it would be as well not to mention the subject. They did not delay long at the meal, but hastened back to their self-imposed task.

"Now let's hurry up and finish the altar," said Abby.

Having completed the adornment of the table, by throwing over the muslin a fine lace curtain, from the linen press also, and decking it with some artificial flowers found in her mother's wardrobe, Abby brought the statue from the parlor, and set it upon the shrine which she and Larry had taken so much trouble to prepare. Larry placed before the lovely image his little vase containing a small bunch of dandelions he had gathered in the yard. He was particularly fond of dandelions. Abby had nothing to offer but her May wreath, which she laid beside it. But the decorations appeared too scanty to satisfy her.

"I'll get the high pink vases from the parlor," said she.

"Yes," added Larry. "And the candlesticks with the glass hanging all round them like a fringe, that jingles when you touch them."

The little girl brought the vases. Then she carried in the candelabra, the crystal pendants ringing as she walked in a way that delighted Larry. She knew perfectly well that she was never allowed to tamper with the costly ornaments in the parlor; but she excused herself by the plea: "I'm doing it for the Blessed Virgin." Larry also had a certain uneasiness about it, but he said to himself: "Oh, it must be all right if Abby thinks so! She is a great deal older than I am, and ought to know."

The shrine was certainly elaborate now. The children were so engrossed with admiring it that they did not hear the house door open and close. A step in the hall, however, reminded the little girl of her music lesson.

"Gracious, that must be Miss Remick!" she said, in confusion.

She quietly opened the door of the oratory, intending to peep into the parlor to see if the teacher was there. To her surprise she encountered her mother, who had just come up the stairs. But Mrs. Clayton was much more astonished by the sight which greeted, her eyes when she glanced into the oratory.

"O Abby," she exclaimed, in distress and annoyance, "how could you be so disobedient! O Larry, why did you help to do what you must have known I would not like?"

Larry grew very red in the face, looked down, and fumbled with one of the buttons of his jacket,

"But, mother," began Abby, glibly, "it was for the Blessed Virgin, you know. I was sure I could put down the carpet all right, and I thought you would be glad to be saved the trouble."

"Put it down all right!" rejoined her mother. "Why, you have ruined the carpet, Abby!"

Both children looked incredulous and astonished.

"Don't you see that you have cut it up so shockingly that it is entirely spoiled? What is left would have to be so pieced that I can not possibly use it for the dining-room, as I intended."

Abby was mortified and abashed. Larry grew more and more uncomfortable.

"And, then, the vases and candelabra!" continued Mrs. Clayton. "Have you not been forbidden to lift or move them, daughter?"

"Yes, mother," acknowledged the little girl. "But I thought you wouldn't mind when I wanted them for the altar. I didn't suppose you'd think anything you had was too good for the Blessed Virgin."

"Certainly not," was the reply. "I had decided to place the candelabra on your little shrine. The pink vases are not suitable. But these ornaments are too heavy for you to carry. It was only a happy chance that you did not drop and break them. And, then, the statue! Do you not remember that I would not permit you to move it yesterday? How would you have felt if it had clipped from your clasp and been dashed to pieces?"

A few tears trickled down Abby's cheeks. Larry blinked hard and stared at the wall.

"My dear children, that is not the way to honor our Blessed Mother," Mrs. Clayton went on to say. "Do you think that she looked down with favor upon your work to-day? No. But if you had waited as I told you, - if each of you had made a little altar for her in your heart and offered to her the beautiful flowers of patience, and the votive lights of loving obedience, -

then indeed you would have won her blessing, and she would have most graciously accepted the homage of such a shrine. As it is, you see, you have very little, if anything, to offer her."

III.

For two or three days Mrs. Clayton suffered the oratory to remain as the children had arranged it. They said their prayers there morning and evening; and to Abby especially the ridges and patches in the carpet, which now seemed to stare her out of countenance, the pink vases, and the candelabra, were a constant reproach for her disobedience. Larry, too, grew to hate the sight of them. He often realized poignantly also that it is not well to be too easily influenced by one's playmates; for if he happened to be late and ran into the room and popped down on his knees in a hurry, he was almost sure to start up again with an exclamation caused by the prick of one of the numerous tacks which he had inadvertently left scattered over the floor.

When the good mother thought that the admonition which she wished to convey was sufficiently impressed, she had the carpet taken up, repaired as much as possible, and properly laid. Then she hung soft lace curtains at the window, draped the altar anew, took away the pink vases, and put the finishing touches to the oratory. It was now a lovely little retreat. Abby and Larry never tired of admiring it. They went in and, out of the room many times during the day; and the image of the Blessed Virgin, ever there to greet them, by its very presence taught them sweet lessons of virtue. For who can look upon a statue of Our Lady without being reminded of her motherly tenderness, her purity and love; without finding, at least for a moment, his thoughts borne upward, as the angels bore the body of the dead St. Catherine, from amid the tumult of the world to the holy heights, the very atmosphere of which is prayer and peace?

Whenever Abby felt cross or disagreeable, she hid herself in the oratory until her ill-humor had passed. This was certainly a great improvement upon her former habit, under such circumstances, of provoking a quarrel with Larry, teasing Delia, and taxing her mother's patience to the utmost. She liked to go there, too, in the afternoon when she came in from play, when twilight crept on and deepened, and the flame of the little altar lamp that her father had given her shone like a tiny star amid the dusk of the quiet room. Larry liked it better when, just after supper, the candles of the candelabra were all lighted, and the family gathered around the shrine and said the Rosary together.

To Abby belonged the welcome charge of keeping the oratory in order; while Larry always managed to have a few flowers for his vase, even if they were only dandelions or buttercups. He and his sister differed about the placing of this offering.

"What a queer boy you are!" said Abby to him one day. "Your vase has a pretty wild rose painted on it, yet you always set it with the plain side out. Nobody'd know it was anything but a plain white vase. You ought to put it round this way," she added, turning it so that the rose would show.

"No, I won't!" protested Larry, twisting it back again. "The prettiest side ought to be toward the Blessed Virgin."

"Oh - well - to be sure, in one way!" began Abby. "But, then, the shrine is all for her, and this is only a statue. What difference does it make which side of the vase is toward a statue? And it looks so funny to see the wrong side turned to the front. Some day we'll be bringing Annie Conwell and Jack Tyrrell, and some of mother's friends, up here; and just think how they'll laugh when they see it."

Larry flushed, but he answered firmly: "I don't care! - the prettiest side ought to be toward the Blessed Virgin."

"But it is only a statue!" persisted Abby, testily.

"Of course I know it is only a statue," replied her brother, raising his voice a trifle; for she was really too provoking. "I know it just as well as you do. But I think Our Lady in heaven understands that I put the vase that way because I want to give her the best I have. And I don't care whether any one laughs at it or not. That vase isn't here so Annie Conwell or Jack Tyrrell or anybody else will think it looks pretty, but only for the Blessed Virgin, - so there!"

Larry, having expressed himself with such warmth, subsided. Abby did not venture to turn the vase again. She was vaguely conscious that she had been a little too anxious to "show off" the oratory, and had thought rather too much of what her friends would say in regard to her arrangement of the altar.

It was about this time that Aunt Kitty and her little daughter Claire came to stay a few days with the Claytons. Claire was only four years old. She had light, fluffy curls and brown eyes, and was so dainty and graceful that she seemed to Abby and Larry like a talking doll when she was comparatively quiet, and a merry, roguish fairy when she romped with them.

"How do you happen to have such lovely curls?" asked Abby of the fascinating little creature.

"Oh, mamma puts every curl into a wee nightcap of its own when I go to bed!" answered the child, with a playful shake of the head.

Larry thought this very droll. "Isn't she cunning?" he said. "But what can she mean?"

"Your mother puts your hair into a nightcap!" cried Abby. "Those are curl papers, I suppose."

"No, nightcaps," insisted the little one. "That's the right name."

The children puzzled over it for some time; but finally Aunt Kitty came to the rescue, and explained that she rolled them on bits of muslin or cotton, to give them the soft, pretty appearance which Abby so much admired; because Claire's father liked her to have curls, and the poor child's hair was naturally as straight as a pipe stem.

"Come and see our chapel, Claire," said Abby; the word oratory did not yet come trippingly to her tongue.

Claire was delighted with the beautiful image, and behaved as decorously as if she were in church. Afterward the children took her to walk. They went into the park, in which there were many handsome flower-pots, several fountains, and a number of fine pieces of marble statuary. Claire seemed to be much impressed with the latter.

"Oh, my!" she exclaimed, pointing to them reverently. "Look at all the Blessed Virgins!"

The children laughed. She stood looking at them with a little frown, not having quite made up her mind whether to join in their mirth, or to be vexed. When her mistake was explained to her, she said, with a pout:

"Well, if they are not Blessed Virgins, then I don't care about them, and I'm going home."

The children had promptly sent a note to Father Dominic thanking him for his appropriate May-Day gift. Each had a share in the composition of this acknowledgment, but it had been carefully copied by Abby. Later they had the satisfaction of showing him the oratory. While Claire was with them, he happened to call again one evening just as the young people were saying good-night.

"Larry," whispered Abby, when they went upstairs and she knelt with her brother and cousin before the little altar, - "Larry, let's say our prayers real loud, so Father Dominic will know how good we've got to be since we've had the lovely statue."

"All right," said Larry, obediently.

They began, Abby leading off in clear, distinct accents, and Larry following in a heavy alto; for his voice was unusually

MARY CATHERINE CROWLEY

deep and sonorous for such a little fellow. Baby Claire listened wonderingly. Then, apparently making up her mind that the clamor was due to the intensity of their fervor, she joined with her shrill treble, and prayed with all her might and main.

To a certain extent, they succeeded in their object. The din of their devotions soon penetrated to the library, where their friend Father Dominic was chatting with Mr. and Mrs. Clayton. In a few moments the latter stepped quietly into the lower hall.

"Abby!" she called, softly.

The little girl pretended not to hear, and kept on.

"Abby!" - there was a decision in the tone which was not to be trifled with.

"What is it, mother?" she asked, with an assumption of innocence, breaking off so suddenly as to startle her companions.

"Not so loud, dear. You can be heard distinctly in the library."

Abby and Larry snickered; Claire giggled without knowing why. Then Abby applied herself with renewed earnestness and volubility to the litany. She did not intend any disrespect: on the contrary, she meant to be very devout. But she not only believed in the injunction "Let your light shine before men," but felt that it behooved her to attract Father Dominic's attention to the fact that it *was* shining. Clearer and higher rose her voice; deeper and louder sounded Larry's; more shrilly piped Claire.

"Abby!" called Mrs. Clayton again, with grave displeasure. "That will do. Children, go to your rooms at once."

The others stole off without another word, but Abby lingered a minute. Father Dominic was going, and she could not resist the impulse to wait and learn what impression their piety had made. Leaning over the balusters, she saw him laughing in an amused manner. Then he said to her mother:

"Tell Abby she has such a good, strong voice, I wish I could have her read the prayers for the Sodality. She would surely be heard all over the church."

He went away, and Abby crept upstairs with burning cheeks and an unpleasant suspicion that she had made herself ridiculous.

Mrs. Clayton suspected that her little daughter had overheard the message. She therefore spared the children any reference to the subject. But the next time they met Father Dominic he alluded, as if casually, to the devotions suitable for May, and then quite naturally went on to speak of the virtues of the Blessed Virgin, especially of her humility and love of retirement; saying how, although the Mother of God, she was content to lead a humble, hidden life at Nazareth, with no thought or wish to proclaim her goodness from the house-tops. The lesson was gently and kindly given, but Abby was shrewd enough and sufficiently well disposed to understand. She felt that she was indeed learning a great deal during this Month of Mary.

About the middle of the month there was a stir of pleasurable excitement at St. Mary's School.

"Suppose we get up a May drama among the younger pupils?" suggested Marion Gaines, the leading spirit of the graduating class.

The proposition was received with enthusiasm, and Mother Rosalie was applied to for permission.

"Yes," she answered, "you have my consent to your plan; but on one condition - that you arrange the drama and drill the children yourselves. It will be good practice for you in the art of composition; and, by teaching others, you will prove whether or not you have profited by Professor Willet's lessons in elocution."

The Graduates were delighted.

"That is just like Mother Rosalie," said Marion. "She is willing to trust us, and leaves us to our own resources, so that if we succeed all the credit will be ours. Now we must draw up a plan. Shall we decide upon a plot, and then each work out a portion of it?"

"Oh, dear, I never could think of anything!" declared one.

"I should not know how to manage the dialogue. My characters would be perfect sticks," added a second.

"I can't even write an interesting letter," lamented some one else.

"I respectfully suggest that Marion and Ellen be requested to compose the drama," said the first speaker, with mock ceremony.

"I agree with all my heart!" cried one.

"And I," - "and I!" chimed in the others.

"It is a unanimous vote," continued their spokesman, turning to the young ladies in question, with a low bow.

"But we shall have all the work," objected Marion.

"No: we will take a double share at the rehearsals, and they will be no small part of the trouble."

"I'll do it if you will, Ellen," began Marion.

"I don't mind trying," agreed Ellen.

Thus the matter was settled.

"Let us first select the little girls to take part in our drama," Marion continued.

"There's Annie Conwell," said one.

"And Lucy Caryl," interposed another.

So they went on, till they had chosen ten or twelve little girls.

"As it is to be a May piece, of course we must have a Queen," said Ellen.

"Yes; and let us have Abby Clayton for the Queen," rejoined Marion. "Abby is passably good-looking and rather graceful; besides, she has a clear, strong voice, and plenty of self-confidence. She would not be apt to get flustered. Annie Conwell, now, is a dear child; but perhaps she would be timid, and it would spoil the whole play if the Queen should break down."

After school the little girls were invited into the Graduates' class-room; and, although not a word of the drama had yet been written, the principal parts were then and there assigned. Lucy Caryl was to have the opening address, Annie as many lines as she would undertake, and so on.

Abby was delighted to find that she was chosen for the most prominent *role*. She ran all the way home, and skipped gaily into the house and up to the sitting-room, where Mrs. Clayton was sewing.

"O mother!" she exclaimed, tossing off her hat and throwing her books upon the table, "we are to have a lovely drama at our school, and I'm to be the May-Queen!"

IV

"Just think, Larry!" said Abby to her brother, when he came home after a game of ball, "I'm to be Queen of May!"

"You!" he cried, in a disdainful tone.

"Yes, indeed! And why not? I'm sure I don't see why you should look so surprised. I've been chosen because I can speak and act the best in our division."

"But the Blessed Virgin is Queen of May," objected Larry.

"Oh, of course!" Abby said. "But this will be only make believe, you know. We are going to have a drama, and I'm to be Queen, - that is all."

"I should think you would not even want to play at taking away what belongs to the Blessed Virgin," persisted Larry, doggedly. "She is the Queen of May, and no one ought to pretend to be Queen besides."

"Oh, you silly boy! There is no use in trying to explain anything to you!" cried Abby, losing patience.

For the next half hour she was not so talkative, however, and after a while she stole away; for in spite of her petulance at Larry's words, they had suggested a train of thought which made her want to be by herself. She went up to the oratory and stayed there a long time, amid the twilight shadows. Finally the ringing of the supper bell put an end to her musings. She knelt a few minutes before the statue, and then ran down to the dining-room. She was very quiet all the evening; and, to Mrs. Clayton's surprise, the family heard no more of the May drama.

The next day, at school, Abby waylaid Marion Gaines in one of the corridors.

"I want to speak to you," she began.

"Well, what's the matter, Abby? What makes you so serious this morning?" inquired Marion.

"Nothing - only I've been thinking about the May piece, and I want to tell you that I'd rather not be Queen," faltered the little girl,

"You'd rather not be Queen!" repeated Marion, in astonishment. "Why not? I thought you were delighted to be chosen."

"So I was - yesterday," the little girl hastened to say; for she would not have Marion think she did not appreciate the compliment.

"Then what has caused you to change your mind so suddenly?" Marion went on. "What a fickle child you are, to be sure!"

"It is not that," stammered poor Abby, a good deal confused; "but - but - well, you know the Blessed Virgin is Queen of May, and it seems as if we ought not even to play at having any other Queen."

Marion stared at her incredulously. "And so missy has a scruple about it?" she said, smiling.

"No," returned Abby; "but my brother Larry thought so. And if it looks that way even to a little boy like him, I think I would rather not pretend to be Queen."

"A May piece without a Queen! Why, it would be like the play of Hamlet with Hamlet left out!" declared Marion. "Did you not think that if you declined the part we might give it to some one else?"

Abby colored and was silent. This had, indeed, been the hardest part of the struggle with herself. But there was an

MARY CATHERINE CROWLEY

element of the heroic in her character. She never did anything by halves; like the little girl so often quoted, "when she was good, she was very, *very*, good."

Marion stood a moment looking at her. "And do you really mean," she said at length, "that you are ready to give up the *role* you were so delighted with yesterday, and the satisfaction of queening it over your companions if only for an hour? - that you are willing to make the sacrifice to honor the Blessed Virgin?"

With some embarrassment, Abby admitted that this was her motive.

A sudden thought occurred to Marion. "Then, Abby, you shall!" said she. "I'll arrange it; but don't say a word about it to any one. Let the girls think you are to be Queen, if they please. Why, missy," she went on, becoming enthusiastic, "it is really a clever idea for our drama. We shall have a lovely May piece, after all."

Marion hastened away, intent upon working out the new plan which her quick fancy had already sketched in outline. To be sure, she and Ellen had devised a different one, and agreed that each should write certain scenes. Ellen had taken the first opportunity that morning to whisper that she had devoted to the drama all the previous evening and an hour before breakfast. Marion, indeed, had done the same.

"But it will not make any difference. We can change the lines a little," she said to herself, after reading the manuscript, which Ellen passed to her at the hour of German study, - a time they were allowed to take for this particular composition.

Ellen, however, thought otherwise.

"What! another plan for the May piece!" she said, when Marion mentioned the subject. "Why, see all I've written; and in rhyme, too!"

"But it can be altered without much trouble," explained her friend.

"No, it can't. You will only make a hodge-podge of my verses," she answered, excitedly. "I do think, Marion, that once we agreed upon the plan, you ought to have kept to it, instead of changing everything just because of a notion of a little girl like Abby Clayton. Here I've been working hard for nothing, - it was just a waste of time!"

Marion pleaded and reasoned, but without avail. Ellen's vanity was wounded. She chose to imagine that her classmate, and sometimes rival, did not care whether her lines were spoiled or not.

"No, no!" she reiterated. "I'll have nothing to do with your new plan. You can get up the whole piece yourself."

"At least give me what you have written," urged Marion. "We are so hurried, and the children ought to have their parts as soon as possible."

But Ellen remained obdurate.

Marion consulted the others of the class, and, after some discussion, they decided in favor of the later design. For the next few days she devoted every spare moment to the work. By the end of the week she had not only finished the portion she had been expected to write, but also much of what Ellen was to have done; and the parts were distributed among the children. There were still wanting, however, the opening address and a dialogue, both of which Ellen had completed.

"Oh, dear," cried Marion, "that address of Ellen's is so pretty and appropriate! If she would only let us have it! As we planned it together, if I write one the principal ideas will be the same; and then, likely as not, she will say I copied from hers. How shall I manage?"

Ellen remained on her dignity. She would have nothing to do either with Marion or the drama, and kept aloof from her classmates generally.

The intelligence had spread through the school that the two graduates had differed over the May piece. The exact point in dispute was not known, however: for Marion wished to keep her design a secret, and Ellen would not condescend to explain. In fact, she did not clearly understand it herself; for she had been too vexed at the proposal to change the plan to listen to what Marion said upon the subject.

During this state of affairs poor Abby was very unhappy. She felt that she was the cause of all the trouble; and it seemed hard that what she had done with the best of intentions should have made so much ill-feeling. This disastrous occurrence was followed by another, which made her think herself a very unfortunate little girl.

As has already been explained, it was Larry's delight to keep always a few fresh blossoms in his pretty vase before the beloved statue of the Blessed Virgin. This he attended to himself, and no one ever interfered with the vase. On the day referred to Abby had been rehearsing with Marion, and thus it happened that they walked part of the way home together. Marion stopped at a florist's stand and bought a little bunch of arbutus.

"Here, put this on your altar," she said, giving it to Abby. She had heard all about the oratory.

When the little girl reached the house Larry had not yet come in, and the flowers had not been renewed that day.

"I'll surprise him," she said to herself. "How pleased he will be to see this nice little bouquet!"

She took the vase, threw away the withered violets it contained, replaced them with the May-flowers, and put it back. But, alas! being taken up with admiring the delicate pink arbutus, and inhaling its fragrance, she did not notice that she had set the vase in an unsteady position. The next moment it tipped over, fell to the floor, and lay shattered at the foot of the altar. Abby stood and gazed at it hopelessly, too distressed even to gather up the fragments.

"Oh, what will Larry say!" she cried, wringing her hands. "He thought so much of that vase! What shall I do?"

While she was thus lamenting she heard Larry's voice. He was coming straight up to the oratory. In another minute he threw open the door; he had a little cluster of buttercups in his hand, and was so intent upon putting them in the vase that he was half-way across the room before he noticed the broken pieces on the floor. When he did so, he stopped and glared at his sister.

"O Larry," she stammered, contritely, "it was an accident! See! Marion Gaines gave me those lovely May-flowers, and I thought you'd be pleased to have them in your vase. Just as I went to put it back, it fell over. I'm awfully sorry!"

Larry's eyes flashed angrily, and his face grew crimson.

"Abby Clayton," he broke out, "you are always meddling! Why can't you let things that don't belong to you alone?"'

A storm of reproaches would no doubt have followed, but just then his angry glance turned toward the statue. There stood the image of Our Lady, so meek and beautiful and mild. And there, in a tiny frame at the front of the altar, hung father Dominic's words of advice: "Try every day to do some little thing to honor our Blessed Mother."

Larry paused suddenly; for his indignation almost choked him. But in that moment of silence he had time to reflect. What should he do to-day to honor the Blessed Virgin, now that his little vase was broken? He looked again at the statue. The very sight of the sweet face suggested gentler thoughts, and counselled kindness, meekness, and forbearance.

"Well, Abby," he blurted out, "I suppose I'll have to forgive you; but, oh, how I wish I were only six years old, so that I could cry!"

So saying, Larry laid the buttercups at the feet of Our Lady's statue, and rushed from the room.

The next day it happened that Ellen discovered Abby in tears at the window of the class-room. Ellen, although quick-tempered and impulsive, was kind-hearted.

"What is the trouble now, child?" she asked, gently, taking Abby's hand in hers.

"Oh," sobbed Abby, "I feel so dreadfully to think that you and Marion don't speak to each other! And it's all my fault; because from something I said to Marion she thought that, instead of taking one among ourselves, it would be much nicer to choose the Blessed Virgin for our May-Queen."

"And was that Marion Gaines' plan?" asked Ellen, in surprise.

"Why, yes! But surely she must have told you!" said the little girl.

"I see now that she tried to," replied Ellen, with a sigh at her own impetuosity. "But I was too vexed to listen. I did not really understand before. Dry your tears, Abby; I'll do my best to make amends now. How foolish I've been!" she ejaculated, as Abby ran off in gay spirits. "And how I must have disedified the other girls! I must try to make up for it."

She found the verses she had written; and, on looking them over, concluded that, after all, they needed only the change of a few words here and there. Then she wrote a little note to Marion, as follows:

"DEAR MARION: - I did not realize until today what you wanted to do about the May piece. If my verses would be of any use at this late hour, you are welcome to them. I should like to do all I can to help now, to make up for lost time."

"ELLEN."

Marion gladly accepted the overtures of peace. The May drama was duly finished, the rehearsals went on smoothly, and on the last day of the Month of Mary the performance took place.

It had been rumored in the school that Abby was not to be Queen, and there was much speculation as to which of the little girls had been selected instead. As the drama progressed, and the plan was unfolded, the audience was taken completely by surprise. Everyone had been eager to see the May-Queen; but there was a general murmur of appreciation when, at the close, the curtain rose upon a beautiful tableau; a shrine glittering with many lights, in the midst of which was enthroned a lovely image of Our Lady, at whose feet the children laid their crowns of flowers - a crown to honor each transcendent virtue, - and paid their homage to their beautiful Queen of May.

A few days later Father Dominic called at the Claytons.

"Well, children," he asked, incidentally, "have you done anything to please the Blessed Virgin during the past month?"

Abby and Larry were silent, but their mother kindly answered:

"I think they have tried, Father Dominic. And as for your lovely May-Day gift, the presence of the statue seems to have drawn down a blessing upon the house."

TILDEREE

I.

Quite happy indeed was the home of Tilderee Prentiss, though it was only a rough log house on a ranch, away out in Indian Territory. Her father was employed by the owner of the ranch. He had, however, a small tract of land for himself, and owned three horses and several cows. Her mother's duties included the management of a small dairy and poultry yard, the products of which were readily sold at the military post some miles distant.

There were two other children: Peter, thirteen years old; and Joanna, or Joan as she was called, who had just passed her eleventh birthday. They took care of the fowl, and were proud when at the end of the week they could bring to their mother a large basket of eggs to carry to the Fort.

The only one of the family who could afford to do nothing was six-year-old Tilderee, though they thought she did a good deal - that is, all except Joan; for she seemed to make everybody's else burden lighter by her merriness, her droll sayings, and sweet, loving little ways.

Yet she was continually getting into mischief; and to see her trotting to and fro, eager to be of use, but always lending a little hindering hand to everything, one would hardly consider her a help. "How should I ever get on without the child!" her mother would often exclaim; while at the same moment Tilderee might be dragging at her gown and interfering with her work at every step.

How frequently Mrs. Prentiss laughed, though with tears in her eyes, as she thought of the time when Tilderee, a toddling baby, was nearly drowned by tumbling head-foremost into a pailful of foaming milk, and no one would have known and rushed to save her but for the barking of the little terrier Fudge! Then there was the scar still to be found beneath the soft ringlets upon her white forehead, a reminder of the day when she tried to pull the spotted calf's tail. How frightened "papa" was at the discovery that his mischievous daughter had been at his ammunition chest, played dolls with the cartridges, and complained that gunpowder did not make as good mud pies as "common dirt!"

Peter and Joan could add their story, too. Peter might tell, for instance, how Tilderee and Fudge, the companion of most of her pranks, frightened off the shy prairie-dogs he was trying to tame; saying they had no right to come there pretending to be dogs when they were only big red squirrels, which indeed they greatly resembled. Still he was very fond of his little sister. He liked to pet and romp with her, to carry her on his back and caper around like the friskiest of ponies. When he paused for breath she patted his sun-burned cheek with her dimpled hand, saying, in her cooing voice, "Good brother Pippin!" which was her nickname for him. Then he forgot that she delighted to tease him, - that her favorite pastime was to chase the young chicks and cause a tremendous flutter in the poultry yard; and how vexed he had been when she let his mustang out of the enclosure, "because," she said, "Twinkling Hoofs needs a bit of fun and a scamper as well as anybody; and he was trying to open the gate with his nose." It took two days to find the mustang and coax him back again. Tilderee was penitent for fully ten minutes after this escapade; but she endeavored to console herself and Peter by declaring, "I know, Pippin, that the Indians must have Twinkling Hoofs by this time. And he's so pretty they'll keep him for a chief to ride; a big, fat chief, with a gay blanket and a feather headdress, and red and blue paint on his face. Won't Twinkling Hoofs be s'prised at all that? But never mind, Pippin; papa will let you ride the old grey horse!"

No one knew better than Joan, however, just how tantalizing Tilderee could be, - how she dallied in the morning playing hide-and-seek, refusing to have her face washed and her tangled hair brushed into shining curls; this, too, when Joan was in the greatest hurry to go and give the fluffy chicks and the grave old fowl their breakfast. It was very well for Peter to say, "What should we do without Tilderee?" If she bothered him he could take his rifle and go shooting with Abe, the old scout; or jump upon Twinkling Hoofs and gallop all over the ranch. How would he like the midget to tag after him all day, to have the care of her when mother went to the Fort to sell the butter and eggs? "Indeed I could get on very well without the little plague," Joan sometimes grumbled - "just for a *teenty* bit of a while," she generally added, hastily; for she really loved her little sister dearly. Joan tried hard to be patient, but she had a quick temper, and occasionally forgot her good resolutions. This happened one day when her mother had gone to dispose of the dairy products. The provocation was certainly great.

Joan had a lovely French doll - the only French doll in the Territory, and probably the most beautiful one to be found within many hundred miles. Mrs. Miller, the wife of one of the officers at the Fort, brought it to her from Chicago; and the little girl regarded it as more precious than all the family possessions combined. What, then, was her consternation this morning to see Fudge dash around the corner of the house dangling the fair Angelina by the blue silk dress, which he held between his teeth, and Tilderee following in wild pursuit! Joan rushed out and rescued her treasure; but, alas! it was in a sadly dilapidated condition. She picked up a stick and started after the dog, but Tilderee interfered.

"Oh, please, dear Joan!" she cried, holding her back by the apron strings. "Fudge isn't the most to blame. I took Angelina. I s'pose he pulled off the wig and broke the arm, but I pushed the eyes in; didn't mean to, though - was only trying to make them open and shut. Tilderee's so sorry, Joan!"

The explanation ended with a contrite sob and what Mr. Prentiss called "a sun shower." But the sight of the child's tears, instead of appeasing, only irritated Joan the more. Giving her a smart shake, she said excitedly:

"Tilderee Prentiss, you're a naughty, naughty girl! I wish you didn't live here. I wish mother had let you go with the lady at the Fort who wanted to adopt you. I wish I hadn't any little sister at all!"

Tilderee stopped crying, and stood gazing at the angry girl in astonishment; then, swallowing a queer lump that came in her throat, she drew herself up with a baby dignity which would have been funny but for the pathetic expression of her sweet face, as she lisped slowly: "Very well. P'rhaps some day Tilderee'll go away and never come back again!"

She turned and went into the house, with Fudge at her heels. As he passed Joan his tail, which had drooped in shame at his conduct, erected itself defiantly, and he uttered a growl of protest.

Joan remained disconsolately hugging and weeping over the ill-fated Angelina. But, somehow, she did not feel any better for having yielded to her anger. "Tilderee deserved a good scolding," she said to herself over and over again. Still there was a weight upon her heart, not caused by the ruin of the doll; for, notwithstanding all the excuses she could muster, her conscience reproached her for those unkind, bitter words. After a while, remembering that she had been cautioned not to let Tilderee out of her sight, she started to look for her. The culprit was soon discovered in the corner of the kitchen cupboard, which she called-her "cubby-house," engaged in lecturing Fudge for running away with Angelina.

"Never meddle with what does not belong to you!" she said, laying down the law with her mite of a forefinger; and, to make her words more impressive, giving him an occasional tap on the nose. He listened dutifully, as if he were the sole transgressor; but interrupted the homily now and then by lapping the hand of his little mistress with his tiny red tongue, as a token of the perfect understanding between them.

When they looked up and saw Joan, both glanced at her deprecatingly, but quite ready to assume a defensive attitude. Ashamed of having allowed her indignation to carry her so far, she was, however, inclined to be conciliatory; and therefore, with an effort, managed to say, as if nothing had happened:

"Come, Tilderee! Watch at the window for father, while I get dinner ready."

Tilderee at once sprang to her feet gaily, threw her arms around Joan's waist, and held up her rosy mouth for the kiss of mutual forgiveness, Fudge wriggling and wagging his tail.

Joan now busied herself about the mid-day meal, for which her mother had made the principal preparation before setting out. She said nothing about the tragedy of the morning when her father came in, partly because she felt that nobody could appreciate the depth of her grief but mother, and because she had made up her mind not to complain of Tilderee, - a conclusion which she secretly felt entitled her to rank as a heroine. But Tilderee related the occurrence herself as soon as her mother returned.

"Fudge and me broke Joan's beauty doll. We didn't mean to, and we're awful sorry, - honest and true we are!"

"But that will not mend Angelina," said Mrs. Prentiss, gravely.

Tilderee hung her head. She now realized for the first time, that no matter how grieved we are, we can not always repair the wrong we have done. The mother, though a plain, uneducated woman, had plenty of good sense, and did her best to train her children well. She now talked very seriously to her little daughter, and Tilderee promised to be less meddlesome and more obedient in the future.

"Fudge and me wants to be good," she said, penitently; "but we forgets. P'rhaps if we were other folks, and our names were something else 'sides Tilderee and Fudge, we might be better."

"I'm afraid Fudge is a hard case," sighed her mother, restraining a smile; "and I should not like to see my little girl changed into any one else. But I expect we ought to call you as you were christened, and that is Matilda. It is a saint's name, you know; and you can pray to your name saint to help you."

The little lass was delighted to have the question settled in this manner, and from that time strove to insist upon her proper title. But it was not easy to drop the pet name, and Tilderee she was oftenest called, till long after the date of this story. For several days she tried very hard to be good; she said her prayers night and morning with special earnestness, always closing with: "Please, God, take care of Tilderee, and keep her and Fudge out of mischief."

Joan, on her part, endeavored to be more gentle with her little sister; for, while every day she lamented the fate of the doll, she could not think of it without feeling a trifle uncomfortable about the way she had spoken to Tilderee.

The two little girls were not allowed to go beyond the enclosure which surrounded the house, unless accompanied by their father or mother. The few Indians in the vicinity had hitherto been peaceable and friendly; but it was considered well to be cautious, and the country was too sparsely settled to render it safe for one to wander about alone. When Mrs. Prentiss, mounted on the old grey horse, rode to the Fort to sell her butter and eggs, Peter went with her on Twinkling Hoofs; and each took the precaution to carry a pistol for self-defence in case of attack.

This being the state of affairs, great was the alarm of all one day as it became evident that Tilderee was missing. The ranch was a scene of intense excitement when, after an exploration of the neighborhood, the child was not found. The news spread like a prairie fire. The settlers for miles around joined the party which set out to continue the search. The poor mother was frantic. The father went about helplessly, like a man dazed by a terrible blow. Peter galloped wildly to and fro upon Twinkling Hoofs, without an idea where he was going. Joan cried as though her heart would break.

Fudge had disappeared also. Had he gone with Tilderee? There was a grain of comfort in the suggestion; yet, even so, what could a poor baby do, astray and with no other defender? Evening came, and still there was no trace of the child. All through the night they continued to seek her, guided by the light of the stars and the glimmer of their pine torches. But in vain.

II.

On that memorable day, shortly after dinner, if mother had not been so absorbed by the discovery that certain wee, blundering fingers had sprinkled sugar instead of salt over her new batch of butter; or if Joan, instead of going for the third time since morning to the lowest drawer of the deal clothes-press which contained the family wardrobe, to take an aggrieved look at Angelina, - if either had glanced out of the doorway, she would have seen a diminutive figure tripping down the trail in happy unconcern, with Fudge gambolling along in front.

Tilderee did not mean to be disobedient: she had no intention of running away; but it was so easy to forget that she had passed the bounds which love had set for her, when the May breezes, like eager playmates, seemed to beset her to frolic with them, catching at her frock, tip-tilting her pretty print sunbonnet (the one with the tiny pink roses scattered over a blue ground), ruffling her chestnut curls, and whisking her little plaid shawl awry. A patch of yellow wild flowers by the way appeared all at once endowed with wings, as from their midst arose a flight of golden butterflies. What fun to chase them! Fudge thought so too, and a merry pursuit followed. Tired and out of breath, Tilderee paused at last. Fudge returned with a bound to her side, and stood panting and wagging his tail, as if to ask: "Well, what shall we play next?" They were now half a mile from home, but neither turned to look back.

"Fudge, I'm going to pick a lovely bouquet for mother," Tilderee confided to him, patting his shaggy head. He sniffed his approval, and trotted after her as she flitted hither and thither culling the bright blossoms. Now she left the lowlands called the prairie, and climbed Sunset Hill in search of prettier posies. Beyond this rocky knoll was an oak wood, from the direction of which came the noise of running water. At the sound Tilderee remembered that she was thirsty. "There must be a brook in yonder," she said. "Come, Fudge, let us go and see." Trampling among the brambles, the little girl pushed on, and soon came to a small stream dashing along over a stony course. Forming an oak leaf into a cup, as she had often seen Joan do, Tilderee dipped it into the clear current; and by this means, and the sips between times which she took up in the hollow of her hand, succeeded in obtaining a refreshing drink; while from the opposite bank Fudge put down his head and took his share with less ceremony.

Tilderee chose a seat upon a log and rested. To amuse herself she broke off pieces of the underbrush and began to strip them of their leaves. "To make horsewhips, you know," she explained, with a teasing glance at Fudge. He understood very well, and shrank away a trifle; but the next minute the baby hands caressed his rough coat, and she added lovingly: "No, no, Fudge! Nobody shall touch such a good dog!" Throwing aside the sticks, she tried to weave the leaves into garlands, as Joan had taught her. The attempt was hardly a success. As the wreath with which Fudge submitted to be crowned speedily fell apart, she concluded that, instead of making a chain for herself, it would be nicer to carry the oak twig for a sun-shade. At present, however, she laid it carefully on the ground beside her flowers, and proceeded to play in the stream, with bits of bark for boats. Fudge enjoyed this too for a while, but soon he grew restless.

All at once the child became aware that the woods had grown darker; the sunlight no longer glanced in among the green boughs; through the foliage she caught a glimpse of the western sky, which was flecked with flame and beryl and amber. Next she realized that it must be a great while since dinner. With the sense of hunger came a feeling of dismay. Where was she, and how should she get home? "It must be most supper time, Fudge," she said, choking down a sob. The little dog looked up into her face with affectionate concern, and thrust his cold nose into her hand, as if to say encoura-gingly: "Trust me, and I will lead you back." He began to sniff the ground; and, having found the scent, endeavored to prevail upon his young mistress to follow his guidance. But Tilderee was sure that she knew best. "No, Fudge," she called; "not that way. This is the right path, I'm sure. Come quick!" Vainly the sagacious animal used all his dumb arts to induce her to rely upon him; vainly he crouched and whined, and begged her to go *his* way. Tilderee obstinately stumbled on in the opposite direction. Fudge laid down and watched her despairingly for a few moments; then, with a sigh almost like that of a human being, he sprang after her. If actions speak louder than words, could he have said more plainly: "Well, if you *will* get lost, I must go with you to take care of you?"

They wandered on, far beyond the source of the stream, emerged from the wood, and strayed along the side of a deep gorge or canon. At every step the surroundings grew wilder, the way more rocky and precipitous. If she had been older, what terrors would have affrighted the child! An appalling dread of the Indians, fear of the wild cattle of the wilderness, the apprehension of countless dangers. But in her baby innocence, Tilderee knew nothing of these perils. She only felt that she was weary and chilled, and faint for want of food. "Oh Fudge, if we could only get home to mother!" she moaned. "Tilderee's so tired and sleepy, and it will be dark night soon." At the thought she threw herself on the ground and began to cry bitterly.

Fudge looked disconsolate. A second he stood irresolute and distressed, but presently drew nearer, and, with unobtrusive sympathy, licked away the salt tears that rolled down her chubby cheeks. Then he roused himself, as if he comprehended that something must be done, and ran to and fro, barking with all his might, and poking about with his nose to the earth. At length he came upon a nook under a projecting rock, which seemed to promise a slight shelter from the cold night air. Perhaps it was the instinct of self-preservation which led him to attract the attention of his helpless companion to it. Several times he returned to her, looked beseechingly into her face, then ran back to the rock.

"You want me to go in there, Fudge?" she faltered at last,

noticing his antics. "Well, I will. P'rhaps it'll be warmer. And I'm afraid nobody'll come now till morning."

Dispirited, Tilderee dragged herself to the refuge he had found. "I 'xpect it's time for night prayers," she said, with a tremor in her voice; "and I always say them with mother or Joan." Now she knelt upon the damp mould, made the Sign of the Cross, and, clasping her brier-scratched hands, repeated the "Our Father" and "Hail Mary" more devoutly than ever before. When she came to the special little petition at the close, "Please, God, take care of Tilderee, and keep her and Fudge out of mischief," she broke down again, and, weeping convulsively, threw her arms around the neck of her obstreperous but loyal playmate and friend, exclaiming, "Oh Fudge! if we ever get safe home we'll never be naughty again, will we?"

Yet exhausted nature stills even the cry of grief and penitence. Tilderee, moreover, felt wonderfully comforted by her prayer. To the pure heart of a child Heaven is ever "close by." From her rude asylum under the cliff the little wanderer looked across at the sky. It was clear and bright with myriad stars. Suddenly one flashed across the broad expanse, blazed from the very zenith, and sped with incredible velocity down, down, till it disappeared in the depths of the ravine. "Ah," said she, with eyes still fixed upon the spot whence had gleamed the meteor, "p'rhaps it was an angel flying down to me! I won't be afraid, 'cause I know God will take care of me." Drawing the small plaid shawl from her shoulders, she spread it over herself like a blanket; sparing a corner for Fudge, however, who stationed himself upon it, prepared to ward off all dangers from his charge. And thus she fell asleep, cheered by the presence and warmed by the breath of the faithful little dog, her sole protector, humanly speaking, in that lonely wilderness.

* * * * *

During the long night, while the searching party was scouring the country, Mrs. Prentiss remained at home, keeping a bright light in the window, a fire on the kitchen hearth, the kettle on the crane, and everything ready to gladden and revive her darling in case, as she persisted in hoping, the dear little rover should, with the aid of fudge, find her way back of her own accord. How many times she started up, thinking she heard the patter of childish feet! How many times she rushed to the door at some sound which to her eager heart seemed like a cry of "Mother!" But Joan, who now kept as close to her as Tilderee was accustomed to do, would murmur sadly, after they had listened a while: "It is only the wind or the call of a bird." At which the unhappy woman, with a great effort to be calm, would sigh: "Let us say the Rosary again." Joan, whose face was stained with tears, and her eyes swollen and red from weeping, responded as best she could between her sobs.

Poor Joan learned in those hours what a terrible punishment is that of remorse. Amid all her thoughts of Tilderee one scene was ever before her: the picture of a rosy culprit, with tangled curls and beseeching eyes, grieved at the mischief she had done, and stammering, "I'm so sorry, Joan!" And then herself, as she snatched up the doll and answered harshly: "You naughty girl! I wish you didn't live here! I wish I hadn't any little sister at all!" Well, her wish had come true: Tilderee was gone. Perhaps she would never live in the log house again. There was no "little plague" to vex or bother Joan now. The lighter chores, which were her part of the housework, could be finished twice as soon, and afterward she would have plenty of time to do as she liked: to play with and sew for Angelina, for instance. Angelina! - how she hated the very name! She never wanted even to see the doll again. Tilderee might get up a "make-believe" funeral, and bury it under the white rosebush. Yes, that would be the prettiest spot; and for old affection's sake the thing should be done properly if she came back, - ah, *if!* And then Joan would put her head down upon the table or a chair, whichever happened to be near, or hide her face in the folds of her apron, and cry: "What *shall* I do without Tilderee! Oh, if God will only give her back to us, I will never say a cross or angry word again!"

Dawn brought no news of the lost child, and the dreary night of suspense was succeeded by a day of anguish. At intervals the seekers sent a message back to the desolate home. Sometimes it was: "Keep up your courage; we trust all will be well." Or, "Though we have not yet found the child, please God we will soon restore her to you," and so on. But, soften it as they could, the fact remained - their expedition had been fruitless: Tilderee was still lost. They at length despaired of gaining trace or tidings of her, and agreed that it was useless to continue the search.

"She must have fallen over a precipice," maintained one of the men.

"If so, we should have met with some sign -" argued another, hesitating at the thought of what that sign might be.

"It is probable that she has been stolen by the Indians," said Lieutenant Miller, of the Fort; "and we must adopt other means to recover her."

Once more dusk was approaching, and they were about to turn back, when - hark! there was a shout from the borders of the canon beyond. A few moments before, Abe, the old scout, had disappeared in that direction. As he pressed onward he presently discovered that, in a wavering line, the brambles seemed to have been recently trodden down. A little farther on, almost hidden among the briers and dry leaves, lay a withered wild flower, like those that grew in the plain below; and farther still, caught upon a bush, was a bit of the fringe of a shawl, so small that it might have escaped any but his "hunter's eye." As he stood still, with senses alert, he heard a sound amid the brush; and, turning quickly, saw that which made him send forth the ringing halloo to his comrades. It was a little dog crawling down toward a hollow, where a spring of water gushed from the ground.

"Fudge!" he called, softly. The dog started, fawned upon him with a low whine; and, with many backward glances to make sure that he was following, led the way to a high rock which shelved inward, forming a sort of canopy above the bank. There, in the rude recess, as he felt confident would be the case, was the lost child. At first he feared she might be dead, so pale and motionless she lay; but when he whispered gently, "Tilderee!" the white eyelids fluttered, then unclosed; the dull eyes lighted up in recognition, and she smiled a wan, weak little smile. Once more Abe's cheery voice rang out, calling, "Found! found!" and the woods and cliffs made merry with the echoes. His companions hastened toward the ravine; but he met them half way, carrying the little one in his arms.

What a shout of joy greeted the sight! What a feeling of thankfulness filled each heart! Mr. Prentiss, strong man though he was, at the relaxing of the terrible tension, fainted like a woman. For a second Peter felt his brain in a whirl, then he leaped upon Twinkling Hoofs, whom he had been leading by the bridle, breathed a word in the ear of the clever mustang, and sped away like the wind, "to tell them at home." Who could describe the emotions of the fond mother when, half an hour later, she clasped her darling to her breast?

What a happy stillness reigned in the house for hours, while Tilderee was tenderly brought back from the verge of starvation! In the beginning she was too feeble to speak; but after a while Mrs. Prentiss noticed that she wanted to say something, and, bending over her, caught the tremulous words: "Oh mother, I'll never be disobedient any more!" It was then that the good woman, who, as the saying is, "had kept up" wonderfully, was overcome, and wept unrestrainedly.

As for Joan, it seemed to her that there could never be any mourning or sadness again. When she had done everything possible for Tilderee, she lavished attentions upon Fudge, and announced to him that henceforth he was to be called Fido (faithful); at which he wagged his tail, as if he found the *role* of hero quite to his liking. Joan's heart was so light that she wished everyone in the world could share her happiness; but

MARY CATHERINE CROWLEY

whether she laughed or chattered, or hummed a little song to herself, the refrain of all this gladness was "Oh, how good God is! How good God is!"

A LITTLE WHITE DRESS

"Only three weeks more, Constance. Aren't you glad?" said Lillie to her little companion and neighbor as they hurried to school.

"Indeed I am. But it's so long in coming!" sighed Constance. "The days never seemed to go so slowly before."

"I have made a calendar, and every morning I cross off a date; there are already seven gone since the 1st of May," explained Lillie, with a satisfied air, as if she had discovered the secret of adding "speed to the wings of time." "We shall not have a great while to wait now."

Was it a grand holiday that our young friends were anticipating so eagerly, or the summer vacation, now drawing near? One might suppose something of the kind. But not at all. On the approaching Feast of the Ascension they were to make their First Communion; and, being convent-bred little girls, every thought and act had been directed to preparation for this great event, to which they looked forward with the artless fervor natural to innocent childhood. No one must imagine, however, that they were diminutive prudes, with long faces. Is not a girl or boy gayest when his or her heart has no burden upon it? In fact, it would have been hard to find two merrier folk, even upon this bright spring morning.

Lillie was a sprightly creature, who, somehow, always reminded Sister Agnes of one of the angels in Murillo's picture, "The Immaculate Conception," - a lively, happy-go-lucky, rollicking angel, who plays hide-and-seek among the folds of Our Lady's mantle, and appears almost beside himself with the gladness of heaven's sunlight. Yet Lillie was by no means an angel. She had her faults of course, and these often sadly tried the patience of the good Sister. She was quick-tempered, volatile, inclined to be a trifle vain. Alas that it is so hard to keep a child's heart like a garden enclosed as with a fragrant hedge, laden with the blossoms of sweet thoughts, - safely shut in from the chilling winds of worldliness! She was lovable withal, generous, affectionate, and would make a fine woman if properly trained.

Constance, a year older, was more sedate, though with plenty of quiet fun about her. But, as a general thing, she knew when to be serious and when to play, - a bit of wisdom which Sister Agnes frequently wished she could manage to impart to the others of the band of aspirants, of whom the gentle nun had special charge.

Constance and Lillie were nearly always together. Now, as they tripped, onward, they were as happy as the birds in the trees above them, and their voices as pleasant to hear. Having turned the corner, they began to meet a company of children, who came along, sometimes in groups, again in detachments of twos and threes, all clad in white, with white veils upon their heads and floating about them as they passed joyously on, as if keeping time to the music of their own happy hearts. Poor children they were, most of them, with plain, ordinary faces, but upon which now shone a light that made one think of old sweet stories, - of St. Ursula and her throng of spotless maidens; of Genevieve, the child-shepherdess of Nanterre. Who that has ever witnessed such a scene can forget it! - this flock of fair, spotless doves amid the dust or mire of the city streets, that by their very passing bring even to the indifferent spectator a thought above gain or traffic, - a memory perhaps of guileless days and noble aspirations, as, looking up at the blue, calm sky, perchance he likens them to the snowy cloud-lets that gather nearest to the sun and are irradiated by its brightness.

"Why," exclaimed Constance, "here come the first communicants of St. Joseph's parish! They must be just going home from Mass. How happy they all are, and how pretty in their white dresses!"

"They do look lovely," assented Lillie, readily. "How could they help it? And some of the dresses are nice, but surely you see, Connie, that others are made of dreadfully common material, and the veils are coarse cotton stuff."

"Well, I suppose they couldn't afford any better," returned Constance, regretfully.

"I declare there's Annie Brogan, whose mother works for us! - don't you know?" cried Lillie, darting toward a girl who had parted with several others at a cross-street and was walking on alone.

As Constance did know, she hastened to greet her, and to vie with Lillie in congratulating her. "O Annie, what a happy day for you!" - "What a favored girl you are!" - "I almost envy you!" - "We have three whole weeks to wait yet!" This is about what they said, again and again, within the next few minutes; while Annie turned from one to the other, with an added gentleness of manner, a smile upon her lips, and a more thoughtful expression in her grey eyes.

Yes, she was happy; she felt that this was indeed the most beautiful day of her life. To be almost envied, too, by such girls as Lillie Davis and Constance Hammond! This was almost incredible; and so she continued to smile at them, putting in a word now and then, while they chattered on like a pair of magpies, and all three were in perfect sympathy.

Presently Lillie chanced to glance at the little communicant's white gown, which, though fresh and dainty as loving hands could make it, was unmistakably well worn, and in some places had evidently been carefully darned; indeed, her sharp eyes discovered even a tiny tear in the skirt, as if Annie had unwittingly put her fingers through it when searching for the pocket.

"Why, Annie Brogan," she exclaimed, thoughtlessly, "you did not wear that dress to make your First Communion!"

"Yes, to be sure. Did not mother do it up nicely?" answered Annie, with naive appreciation of the patient, painstaking skill which had laid the small tucks so neatly, and fluted the thin ruffles without putting a hole through them. "And mother was saying, when she was at work on it, how thankful we ought to be to have it; since, much as she wished to buy a dress for me, she would not have been able to do so, with the rent and everything to pay; and how good your mamma was to give it to me."

"Pshaw!" rejoined Lillie. "I could have given you a dress ten times better than that if I had only remembered. Mamma just happened to put that in with a bundle of some of my last summer's clothes, which she hoped Mrs. Brogan might find useful. But she never dreamed you would wear it to-day."

"I thought it was so nice!" said Annie, coloring, while a few tears of chagrin and disappointment sprang to her eyes; somehow, a shadow seemed to have unaccountably arisen to dim the brightness of this fairest of days, - a wee bit of a shadow, felt rather than defined.

"So it is nice!" declared Constance, frowning at impulsive Lillie, to warn her that she had blundered. "It is ironed perfectly; your mother has made it look beautiful. And what a pretty veil you have!"

"Yes, I did buy that," replied Annie, in a more cheerful tone.

"Oh, it's all right! And Our Lord must have welcomed you gladly, Annie, you are so good and sweet," added Lillie. "I didn't mean any harm in noticing your dress; it was only one of my stupid speeches."

Lillie looked so sorry and vexed with herself that Annie laughed. The shadow was lifted; the children wished one another good-bye; Annie went homeward, while the others quickened their pace, fearing that they would be late for school.

But the circumstance had made an impression, especially upon Lillie; and at the noon recreation, which the first communicants spent together, she hastened to tell her companions about it.

"Just imagine!" she cried; "Annie Brogan made her First Communion this morning, and she wore an old dress of mine, - an old dress, all mended up, that mamma gave her!"

"The idea!" - "What was she thinking of?" etc., etc.; such were the exclamations with which this announcement was greeted. Most of the girls did not know in the least of whom Lillie was speaking, but it was the fact which created such a sensation.

"Why didn't she get a new one?" inquired Eugenia Dillon, a girl of a haughty disposition, who attached a great deal of importance to costly clothes.

"Hadn't any money," responded Lillie, nibbling at a delicious pickled lime which she had produced from a corner of her lunch basket.

"Then I'd wait till I had -"

"Oh, not put off your First Communion!" protested one of the group.

"Why, yes," returned Eugenia, conscious that she had scandalized them a little and trying to excuse herself. "It is not respectful or proper not to be fitly dressed for such a great occasion."

"But Annie was as neat as could be," said Constance; "and

MARY CATHERINE CROWLEY

looked as pretty as a picture, too. I'm sure Our Lord was as pleased with her as if she were dressed like a princess, because she is such a good little thing."

"Come, Connie, don't preach!" objected Eugenia, impatiently. "Besides, how could she have looked pretty in a mended dress? I wish you could see the one I'm going to have! It's to be of white silk, - the best that can be got at Brown's."

"It won't be any more beautiful than mine. I'm to have tulle," said Lillie.

"And I -" continued Constance.

"Mine is to be trimmed with point-lace," broke in another.

"And I'm to wear mamma's diamonds," boasted somebody else.

"You can't," demurred a quiet girl, who had not spoken before. "Sister Agnes said that we are not to be allowed to wear jewelry or silk either; and that, though the material for the dresses may be of as fine a quality as we choose, they ought not be showy or elaborate."

"That is all very well to say," answered Eugenia. "The nuns can enforce these rules in their boarding-schools, but hardly in a day-school like this. We'll wear what we please, or what our mothers select. Mamma has decided to get the white silk for me, because so many of our friends will be present, and she wants my dress to be the handsomest of any."

This information was received without comment, but it aroused in some foolish little hearts a feeling of envy, and in others a desire of emulation.

Eugenia Dillon was the richest girl in the school. Her father, a plain, sensible man, who had lacked early advantages, had within a few years amassed a considerable fortune, which he would gladly have enjoyed in an unostentatious, unpretending manner. This, however, did not suit his wife at all. Mrs. Dillon, though a kind-hearted, charitable woman, was excessively fond of style, lavishly extravagant, and inclined to parade her wealth upon all occasions. She did not realize that the very efforts she made to attain the position in society which would have come to her naturally if she had but the patience to wait, caused her to be sneered at as a *parvenu* by those whose acquaintance she most desired. Unconscious of all this, she pursued her way in serene self-satisfaction, - a complacency shared by Eugenia, who delighted in the good fortune and bad taste which permitted her to wear dresses of silk or velvet to school every day in the week, and caused her to be as much admired as a little figure in a fashion-plate by those of her companions who were too unsophisticated to know that vain display is a mark of vulgarity.

"Oh children, children!" exclaimed Sister Agnes, who caught the drift of the conversation as she came into the room. "Do not be troubling your precious little heads about the fashions. We must all trust something to the good sense of your mammas that you will be suitably gowned. Certainly it is eminently fitting that one should be beautifully attired to honor the visit of the King of kings. Considered in this light, no robe could be too rich, no ornament too splendid. But, lest a small thought of vanity should creep in to spoil the exalted motive, the custom is to adopt a lovely simplicity. If you notice, we never think of the angels as weighed down with jewels. Bestow some of this anxiety upon the preparation of your hearts; see that you are clothed in the royal robes of grace; deck yourself with the jewels of virtue, - rubies for love, emeralds for hope, pearls for contrition, diamonds for faith, and purity. It was with gems like these that the holy maidens, Saints Agnes, Philomena, and Lucy, chose to adorn themselves, rather than with the contents of their trinket caskets."

Thus the nun continued to speak to the band of little girls, who had eagerly gathered around her; thus was she wont to teach them lessons of wisdom in a sprightly, gay, happy-hearted way, as if generosity, unselfishness and self-denial were the most natural traits imaginable, and the whole world fair because it is God's world, and we are all His children. Was it this spirit of joyousness which attracted young people especially to her, and gave her such an influence with them?

"Somehow, when Sister Agnes talks to me," even so flighty a little personage as Lillie Davis said one day, "I feel as if I could make any sacrifice quite as a matter of course, and without a speck of fuss about it."

"Yes," agreed Connie. "She seems to take your hand in her strong one and to lead you up a stony, hilly path; and then, when you come to the roughest, steepest places, she almost carries you onward; and you are ashamed to complain that you are tired, because, though she is so gentle with you, she does not mind such trifles at all herself -"

"She makes me think," interrupted Lillie, "of the pleasant, sunshiny breeze that comes up sometimes on a cloudy morning, and chases away the mists through which everything looks so queerly, and lets us see things as they really are."

Lillie's quaint comparison was an apt one, as was proved in the present instance.

When Sister Agnes had gone the subject which the girls had been discussing presented a different aspect, and the keynote of her character which always impressed them - "Do noble deeds, not dream them all day long," - caused them now to feel dissatisfied with themselves and to cast about for something to do. This reminded Constance again of Annie Brogan and the white dress that Lillie had regarded with so much scorn.

"Girls," said she, "wouldn't it be nice if we could give a dress and veil, and whatever is necessary, to some poor child who is to make her First Communion on the same day as ourselves? Perhaps, too, we could arrange to have her make it with us. Don't you think this would make us happy, and be a good way to prepare?"

"It's a grand idea, Connie!" proclaimed Lillie, with ready enthusiasm.

"How could we do it?" asked the quiet girl, coming to the practical question at once.

"By giving up some of our ribbons and candies and knickknacks during the next few weeks, maybe," continued Constance earnestly, thinking it out as she went along. "Suppose we all agree to get the pretty dresses the nuns wish us to wear on that day, instead of the showy ones we want? They would not cost as much, and our mothers would, I am sure, let us use the extra money in this way."

"What! give up the white silk! Oh, I couldn't!" objected Eugenia, disconcerted. "Anyhow, I don't believe mamma would like to have me do it."

"Tulle is so lovely!" sighed Lillie. "And I never did like plain mull."

On the whole, the proposal was not received with favor. It was discussed with much animation, but the bell rang before any decision had been arrived at. Later, however, after a consultation with Sister Agnes, who promised her cordial co-operation, the children concluded to adopt Connie's suggestion, if their mothers would consent.

"I must acknowledge that I am disappointed," remarked Mrs. Davis to her husband that evening. "To-day I ordered the material for Lillie's First Communion dress, - an exquisite tulle. But she came home from school with a story about furnishing an outfit for a poor child, and she assures me that her companions are to wear plain dresses for the occasion." Thereupon the lady proceeded to give the details of the plan as she had understood it.

"A very creditable determination," said Lillie's papa, approvingly. "I endorse it heartily. If attired simply, the children will not be distracted by the thought of their gowns, while at the same time some deserving little girl will be provided with an appropriate costume. I advise you to send back the tulle by all means, my dear, and apply the difference in price between it and the fabric agreed upon to the fund the children are trying to make up."

"Well, I suppose it will be best to do so," decided his wife. "Anyhow, tulle is so delicate a tissue, and Lillie is such a heedless little creature, that it would probably be badly torn before the end of the ceremonies."

"I am sorry," soliloquized Connie's mother when she heard of the project. "Connie's First Communion will be so important an event for her that I feel as if I could not do enough in preparation for it. I should like to dress her more beautifully than on any day in her life. If she were grown and about to enter society, or if I were buying her wedding-dress, I would select the handsomest material procurable, - why not now, for an occasion so great that I ought hardly mention it in comparison? But, after all," mused she, later, "the children's arrangement is the best. I am happy that Constance is so free from frivolity, and has shown so edifying a spirit."

For Eugenia Dillon, the giving up of the white silk was, as the girls generously agreed, "the biggest act of all." At first Mrs. Dillon would not hear of it; "though," said she, "I am quite willing to buy the dress for the poor child myself, if you wish, Eugenia." But Eugenia explained that this would not do, unless she carried out the plan like the others. In fact, she found that one of the hardest things in the world is to argue against what we want very much ourselves. At last, however, her mother good-naturedly yielded the point, saying, with a laugh, "Oh, very well, child! But I never before knew you to object to having a pretty dress." And Eugenia was very sure she never had.

The great day finally arrived. To picture it, or to describe the joy which filled the soul of each of our first communicants, is not the purpose of this story. But as the white-robed band entered the convent chapel, to the incongruous throng of fashionable people there assembled their appearance was the strongest possible sermon against vanity. Their soft white gowns were as simple as the most refined taste could make them, and as beautiful; their fleecy veils enfolded them as with holy thoughts; their wreaths of spotless blossoms signified a fairer crown. They numbered seven originally, but now among them walked another. Which little girl was the stranger, however, only one mother knew, - a humble woman, who, as she knelt amid the congregation, silently invoked a blessing upon the children who by their thoughtfulness had made possible her pious desire that her child might be appropriately and respectfully attired to welcome the coming of Our Lord.

The first communicants remained at the convent till dusk. During the afternoon somebody noticed, indeed, that Eugenia's dress, though of mull like the rest, was more fanciful, and her satin sash twice as wide as that of any one else. But the discovery only caused a smile of good-humored amusement; for it was hardly to be expected that Eugenia would conform absolutely to the rule they had laid down for themselves.

After Benediction, as they prepared to go home, they said to one another: "What a truly happy day this has been! How often we shall think of it during our lives!"

A MISER'S GOLD

I.

"Never mind, mother! Don't fret. We'll get on all right. This little house is much more comfortable than the miserable flat we have been living in. The air is good, and the health of the children will be better. It is quite like having a home of our own again. Now that Crosswell & Wright have raised my wages, we shall be able to make both ends meet this winter, - you'll see!"

"Yes, dear, I'm sure we shall," Mrs. Farrell forced herself to respond, though her tone did not express the absolute conviction which the words implied. But Bernard was in great spirits, and for his sake she assumed a cheerfulness which she was far from feeling, as she bade him good-bye, and from the window watched him hasten away to his work.

"God bless his brave heart!" she murmured. "He is a good boy and deserves to succeed. It worries me that he has such a burden upon his young shoulders; but Father Hamill says this will only keep him steady, and will do him no harm if he does not overtax his strength. What a shabby, contracted house this is! Well, I must try to make it as bright and pleasant as possible. I wish the girls were older and able to earn a trifle; every penny helps nowadays. Mary, indeed, might find a place to run errands for a dressmaker, or something of the kind; but I can not bear to think of her going around alone down town, becoming pert and forward. Besides, she is so bright and smart that it seems a pity to interfere with her studies. She will need all the advantages she can get, poor child!"

With a sigh the mother returned to her duties, prepared breakfast for the other children and in the course of an hour hurried them off to school. There were three: Mary, just twelve years old; Lizzie, ten; and Jack, who had attained the precocious and mischief-loving age of seven. Bernard was eighteen, and the head of the family, - a fact which Mrs. Farrell strove to impress upon the minds of the younger members, as entitling him to special respect and affection. He was also the principal bread-winner, and had ten dollars a week, which was considered a fine beginning for one so young. Still, it was not a great deal for them all to rely on, and his mother endeavored to eke out their scanty livelihood by taking sewing, and in various other ways.

Life had not always been such a struggle for the Farrells. Before the death of the husband and father they had been in good circumstances. Mr. Farrell held for years a responsible position as book-keeper and accountant in one of the largest mercantile establishments of the city. He had a fair salary, which enabled him to support his family comfortably. But, alas! how much often depends upon the life and efforts of one person! An attack of pneumonia, the result of a neglected cold, carried him out of the world in three days. There had been only time to attend to his religious duties, and no opportunity to provide for the dear ones he was about to leave, even if any provision had been possible. When the income derived from the father's daily labor ceased, they found themselves suddenly plunged into comparative poverty. His life-insurance policy had not been kept up; the mortgage on the pretty home had never been paid off, and was now foreclosed. The best of the furniture was sold to pay current expenses, and the widow removed with her children to the third floor of a cheap apartment house, - one of those showy, aggressively genteel structures so often seen in our Eastern cities, with walls of questionable safety and defective drainage and ventilation.

Mrs. Farrell was now obliged to dismiss her maid-of-all-work, and attend to the household duties herself. This was a hardship, for she was not a strong woman; but she did not complain. Bernard, fortunately, had taken two years of the commercial course at St. Stanislaus' College, and was therefore in a measure fitted for practical affairs. He obtained a place as clerk in the law office of Crosswell & Wright. As he tried to keep his mind on his duties, and was willing and industrious, his employers were well pleased with him, and he had been several times advanced. But the means of the family grew more and more straitened. The following year the rent of the flat was found to be higher than they could afford. They sought other quarters, and settled at last, just as winter was approaching, in the little house where we have discovered them, in a humble neighborhood and unpaved streets, with no pretensions whatever, - in fact, it did not appear to have even the ambition to be regarded as a street at all.

The young people took possession of the new dwelling in high glee. They did not see the drawbacks to comfort which their mother could have pointed out; did not notice how much the house needed painting and papering, how decidedly out of repair it was. Only too glad of their satisfaction, she refrained from comment, tried to make the best of everything, and succeeded in having a cosey home for them, despite all difficulties. For there was not a room of the small house into which at least a ray of sunlight did not find its way sometime during the day. It shone upon threadbare carpets and painted floors; upon sofas the upholstering of which had an unmistakable air of having been experimented with; and chairs which Mrs. Farrell had recaned, having learned the art from a blind boy who lived opposite. Yet the sunlight revealed as well an air of thrift and cheeriness; for the widow, despite her days of discouragement, aimed to train her children to look upon the bright side of life, and to trust in Providence.

"Bernard," said she one evening, "I have been thinking that if I could hire a sewing-machine I might get piecework from the shops, and earn more than by looking to chance patronage. I have a mind to inquire about one."

The boy was silent. She began to doubt if he had heard, and

was about to repeat the remark when he answered:

"No, mother, don't. There are too many women doing that kind of sewing at starvation prices. But I'll tell you what would be a fine thing if you really had the time for it, though I do not see how you could, - it seems to me we keep you busy."

"What is your idea?" inquired Mrs. Farrell eagerly, paying no heed to the latter part of his speech.

"Well, if we could manage to pay the rent of a type-writing machine, I could probably get you copying from the firm as well as from some of the other lawyers in the building. I was wondering the other day if I could do anything at it myself, and thus pick up an additional dollar or two in the week. Of course, you would accomplish more than I could, and it would be a hundred times better than stitch! stitch! How I hate the whir of the thing!" And Bernard, with his juggler gift of mimicry, proceeded forthwith to turn himself into a sewing-machine, jerking his feet up and down in imitation of the motion of the treadle, and making an odd noise in his throat.

Mrs. Farrell laughed, as she replied: "I do not know that there is much choice between this and the click of the type-writer. But, anyhow, your plan, though it sounds plausible, would not do, because I should not be able to work the type-writer."

"There would be no difficulty about that," argued Bernard. "You know how to play the piano, and the fingering is very much easier. It will come naturally."

His mother laughed again, yet she sighed as well. Her father had given her a piano as a wedding present, but this had been the first article of value to be dispensed with when the hard times came. Bernard was so sanguine, however, that she consented to his project. He spoke to Mr. Crosswell on the subject; that gentleman became interested, succeeded in obtaining a type-writer for Mrs. Farrell on easy terms, and promised to send her any extra copying he might have. The manipulation of the machine did not, indeed, come quite as naturally as Bernard predicted, but after a few weeks of patient practice she mastered it sufficiently to produce a neat-looking page. Bernard brought her all the work she could do; it was well paid for, and a more prosperous season seemed to have dawned upon the little home.

Just at this time the children took scarlet fever at school. They had the disease lightly, but what anxiety the mother endured! Thank God, they got through it safely; but there was the doctor's bill to be settled, and funds were at a low ebb once more. To cap the climax, when the house had been thoroughly fumigated by the board of health, and Mrs. Farrell was prepared to take up her occupation again, an attack of rheumatism crippled her fingers and rendered them almost powerless. Then it was that, worn out and disheartened, she broke down and cried:

"Oh! why does not God help us?"

Her son's usually happy face wore an expression of discouragement also as she turned to him with the appeal. His lips twitched nervously; but in a moment the trustfulness which she had taught him was at hand to comfort her.

"Indeed, mother, He will - He *does*," said Bernard tenderly, though in the matter-of-fact manner which he knew would best arouse her. "You are all tired out, or you would not speak in that way. You must have a good rest. Keep the rooms warm, so that you will not take any more cold, and before long you will be able to rattle the type-writer at a greater speed than ever. That reminds me, mother," he continued - seeing that she was beginning to recover herself, and wishing to divert her thoughts, - "one of the things we have to be thankful for is that this house is easily heated. It beats all the way coal does last here! The ton we got two months ago isn't gone yet,"

"That is the way coal lasts when there is not any one to steal it, as there was in the flat, where the cellars were not properly divided off," answered Mrs. Farrell, brightening up.

"No, there's nobody living immediately around here whom I'd suspect of being mean enough to steal coal," returned Bernard, carelessly, - "except, perhaps, Stingy Willis, I don't think I'd wager that old codger wouldn't, though."

"I am afraid I should not have entire confidence in him, either," agreed Mrs. Farrell.

But the intelligence that there was still coal in the bin had cheered her wonderfully. Repenting of her rash conclusion, she hastened to qualify it by adding, "That is, if half of what the neighbors say is true. But, then, we have no right to listen to gossip, or to judge people."

Stingy Willis, the individual who apparently bore an unenviable reputation, was a small, dried-up looking old man, who lived next door to the Farrells, - in fact, under the same roof; for the structure consisted of two houses built together. Here he dwelt alone, and attended to his household arrange- ments himself, except when, occasionally, a woman was employed for a few hours to put the place in order. He was accustomed to prepare his own breakfast and supper; his dinner he took at a cheap restaurant. He dressed shabbily, and was engaged in some mysterious business down town, to and from which he invariably walked; not even a heavy rain-storm could make him spend five cents for a ride in a horse-car. And yet he was said to be very wealthy. Persons declared they knew "upon good authority" that he held the mortgage which covered the two connecting houses; that, as the expression is, he "had more money than he knew what to do with." Others, who did not profess to be so scrupulously exact in their determination to tell only a plain, unvarnished tale, delighted in fabulous stories concerning his riches. They said that though the floor of his sitting-room was carpetless, and the bay- window curtainless but for the cobwebs, he could cover the one with gold pieces and the other with bank-notes, if he pleased. Many were convinced he had a bag of treasure hidden

MARY CATHERINE CROWLEY

up the chimney or buried in the cellar; this they asserted was the reason he would not consent to having the upper rooms of the house rented, and so they remained untenanted season after season. Thus, according to the general verdict (and assuredly the circumstantial evidence was strong), he was a miser of the most pronounced type, - "as stingy as could be," everybody agreed; and is not what everybody says usually accepted as the truth?

Certain it is that Stingy Willis acted upon the principle, "a penny saved is a penny gained," - denied himself every luxury, and lived with extreme frugality, as the man who kept the meat-market and grocery at the corner frequently testified. Even in the coldest weather, a fire was never kindled in the house till evening; for over its dying embers the solitary man made his coffee the following morning. A basket of coal lasted him a week, and he sifted the cinders as carefully as if he did not know where to find a silver quarter to buy more fuel. He had nothing to do with his neighbors, who really knew very little about him beyond what they could see of his daily life. They were almost all working people, blessed with steady employment; though they had not more than enough of this world's goods, there was no actual poverty among them. They were respectable, honest, and industrious; as Bernard said, not one of the dwellers in the street would ever be suspected of being "mean enough to steal coal," unless indeed Stingy Willis.

II.

Gloomy days continued for the Farrells; yet the outside world never dreamed of the straits to which they were reduced, for a spirit of worthy independence and pardonable pride led them to keep their trouble to themselves. Mrs. Farrell would have died, almost, rather than reveal their need to any one; nothing save the cry of her children asking in vain for bread would bring her to it. Well, they still had bread and oatmeal porridge, but that was all.

Who would have imagined it! The little house was still distinguished from the others of the row by an appearance of comfort. Although Mrs. Farrell could not do any type-writing, the children were neat and trim going to school; Bernard's clothes were as carefully brushed, his boots as shining, linen as fresh, his mien as gentlemanly as ever. And they found great satisfaction in the reflection that no one was aware of the true state of affairs. The mother and Bernard agreed, when they began housekeeping under their changed circumstances, to contract no bills; what they could not afford to pay for at the time they would do without. So now no butcher nor baker came clamoring for settlement of his account. The doctor was willing to wait for his money; all they owed besides was the rent. Only the landlord knew this, and he was disposed to be lenient. Mrs. Farrell still tried to hope for the best, but sometimes she grew dejected, was sorely tempted to repine.

"Mother," little Jack once asked, "aren't people who, as you say, 'have seen better days' and become poor, much poorer than people who have always been poor?"

"It seems to me they are, my child," answered the widow, dispiritedly. "But why do you think so?"

"Because," replied the young philosopher, "we are much poorer than he woman who used to wash for us. She appeared to have everything she wanted, but we have hardly anything."

It was unreasonable, to be sure, but sometimes Mrs. Farrell used to wonder how her neighbors could be so hard-hearted as to go past unconcernedly, and not notice the necessities which, all the while, she was doing her best to keep from their knowledge. Often, too, as Stingy Willis went in and out of the door so close to her own, she thought: "How hard it is that this man should have riches hidden away, while I have scarcely the wherewith to buy food for my children! Walls are said to have ears, - why have they not also tongues to cry out to him, to tell him of the misery so near? Is there nothing which could strike a spark of human feeling from his flinty heart?" Then, reproaching herself for the rebellious feeling, she would murmur a prayer for strength and patience.

The partition between the two houses was thin. She and Bernard could frequently hear the old man moving about his dreary apartments, or going up or down the stairs leading to the cellar. "Old Willis is counting his money-bags again, I guess!" Bernard would say lightly, as the familiar shuffling to and fro caught his ear; while his mother, to banish the shadow of envious discontent, quietly told a decade of her Rosary.

The conversation anent the subject of the coal kept recurring to her mind with odd persistency. Repeatedly of late she had awakened in the night and heard the miser stumbling around; several times she was almost certain he was in her cellar, and - yes, surely, *at the coal*, - purloining it piece by piece, probably. Then just as, fully aroused, she awaited further proof, the noise would cease, and she would conclude she must have been mistaken. At last, however, it would seem that her suspicions were confirmed.

On this occasion Mrs. Farrell had not retired at the usual hour. It was after midnight, yet she was still occupied in a rather hopeless effort to patch Jack's only pair of trousers; for he evinced as remarkable an ability to wear out clothes as any son of a millionaire. The work was tedious and progressed slowly, for her fingers were stiff and the effort of sewing painful. Finally it was finished. With a sigh of relief she rested a moment in her chair. Just then the silence was broken by a peculiar sound, like the cautious shifting of a board. That it proceeded from the cellar was beyond question. A singular rattling followed. She rose, went into the hall and listened. Yes, there was no delusion about it: somebody was at the coal, - that coal which, she remembered bitterly, was now but a small heap in the bin. That the culprit was Stingy Willis there could be little doubt.

Bernard had fallen asleep on the sofa an hour or more before. His mother stole to his side, and in a low voice called him. He stirred uneasily. She called again, whereupon he opened his eyes and stared at her in bewilderment.

"Hark!" she whispered, signalling to him not to speak.

Once more came the noise, now more distinct and definable. The heartless intruder had become daring; the click of a shovel was discernible; he was evidently helping himself liberally.

Bernard looked at his mother in perplexity and surprise.

"Stingy Willis?" he interrogated.

She nodded.

"And at the coal, by Jove!" he exclaimed, suddenly realizing the situation, and now wide awake.

He started up, and presently was creeping down the stairs to the kitchen. Mrs. Farrell heard him open the cellar door with the least possible creak. She knew he was on the steps which led below, but he made no further sound. She had no other clue to his movements, and could only distinguish the rumble of the coal. She waited, expecting momentarily that it would cease, dreading the altercation which would follow, and regretting she had aroused her son.

"He is quick-tempered," she soliloquized. "What if words

should lead to blows, - if he should strike the old man! How foolish I was to let him go alone!"

The suspense was ominous. What was the boy going to do? Why all this delay? Why did he not promptly confront the fellow and order him to be gone? In reality, only a few minutes had elapsed since she first heard the noise, but it seemed a quarter of an hour even since he left her. Should she go down herself, or call out to him? While she hesitated Bernard suddenly reappeared. She leaned over the banisters to question him; but, with a gesture imploring her to be silent, the astonished boy said, hardly above his breath: "Mother, come here!"

Cautiously she descended to the entry. He led her through the kitchen to the cellar steps. All the time the shovelling continued. Whispering "Don't be afraid," Bernard blew out the candle he carried, and, taking her hand, added: "Look!"

From the corner of the cellar in which the coal-bin was situated came the light of a lantern. Crouching down, Mrs. Farrell could see that it proceeded from a hole in the wall which separated the two houses. There was no one upon her premises, after all; but at the other side of the partition was Stingy Willis, sure enough! Through the opening she could just catch a glimpse of his grey head and thin, sharp features. Trembling with indignation, she peered forward to get a better view. Yes, there was Stingy Willis certainly; but - oh, for the charity, the neighborliness which "thinketh no evil!" - he was shovelling coal from his own *into* the Farrells' bin! As this fact dawned upon her she felt as if she would like to go through the floor for shame. Drawing back abruptly, she groped her way to the kitchen, and sank into a chair, quite overcome by emotion. Bernard, having relighted the candle, stood gazing at her with an abashed air. In a moment or two the shovelling ceased, and they could hear the old man, totally unconscious of the witnesses to his good deed, slowly ascending to his cheerless rooms again.

Stingy Willis alone had discovered their need. With a delicacy which respected their reticence, and shrank from an offer of aid which might offend, he had hit upon this means of helping them. Clearly, he had been thus surreptitiously supplying them with fuel for weeks, - a little at a time, to avoid discovery. And Mrs. Farrell, in her anxiety and preoccupation, had not realized that, with the steady inroads made upon it, a ton of coal could not possibly last so long.

"That, of all people, Stingy Willis should be the one to come to our assistance!" exclaimed the widow.

"And to think he is not *Stingy* Willis at all! That is the most wonderful part of it!" responded Bernard.

"Often lately," continued the former, "when I happened to meet him going in or out, I fancied that his keen old eyes darted a penetrating glance at me; and the fear that they would detect the poverty we were trying to hide so irritated me that sometimes I even pretended not to hear his gruff 'Good-morning!'"

"Well, he's a right jolly fellow!" cried Bernard, enthusiastically,

His mother smiled. The adjective was ludicrously inappropriate, but she understood Bernard's meaning, and appreciated his feelings as he went on:

"Yes, I'll never let anybody say a word against him in my hearing after this, and I'll declare I have proof positive that he's no miser."

"He is a noble-hearted man certainly," said Mrs. Farrell. "I wish we knew more about him. But, for one thing, Bernard, this experience has taught us to beware of rash judgments; to look for the jewels, not the flaws, in the character of our neighbor."

"Yes, indeed, mother," replied the youth, decidedly. "You may be sure that in future I'll try to see what is best in everyone."

The next morning Mrs. Farrell went about her work in a more hopeful mood. Bernard started for the office in better spirits than usual, humming snatches of a song, a few words of which kept running in his mind all day:

> "God rules, and thou shall have more sun
> When clouds their perfect work have done."

That afternoon Mr. Crosswell, the head of the firm, who seemed suddenly to have become aware that something was wrong, said to him:

"My lad, how is it that your mother has not been doing the extra type-writing lately? I find a great deal of it has been given to some one else."

"She has been sick with rheumatism, sir," answered the boy; "and her fingers are so stiff that she cannot work the machine."

"Tut! tut!" cried the lawyer, half annoyed. "You should have told me this before. If she is ill, she must need many little luxuries" (he refrained from saying *necessaries*). "She must let me pay her in advance. Here are twenty-five dollars. Tell her not to hesitate to use the money, for she can make up for it in work later. I was, you know, a martyr to rheumatism last winter, but young Dr. Sullivan cured me. I'll send him round to see her; and, remember, there will be no expense to you about it."

"I don't know how to thank you, sir!" stammered Bernard, gratefully. Then he hurried home to tell his mother all that had happened, and to put into her hands the bank-notes, for which she could find such ready use.

Doctor Sullivan called to see Mrs. Farrell the following day,

"Why," said he, "this is a very simple case! You would not have been troubled so long but for want of the proper remedies."

He left her a prescription, which wrought such wonders that in a fortnight she was able to resume her occupation.

From this time also Mr. Crosswell gave Bernard many opportunities by which he earned a small sum in addition to his weekly salary, and soon the Farrells were in comfortable circumstances again.

By degrees they became better acquainted with old Willis; but it was not till he began to be regarded, and to consider himself, as an intimate friend of the family that Bernard's mother ventured to tell him they knew of his kind deed done in secret, - a revelation which caused him much confusion. Bernard had discovered long before that their eccentric neighbor, far from being a parsimonious hoarder of untold wealth, was, in fact, almost a poor man. He possessed a life-interest in the house in which he dwelt, and the income of a certain investment left to him by the will of a former employer in acknowledgment of faithful service. It was a small amount, intended merely to insure his support; but, in spite of his age, he still worked for a livelihood, distributing the annuity in charity. The noble-hearted old man stinted himself that he might be generous to the sick, the suffering, the needy; for the "miser's gold" was only a treasure of golden deeds.

THAT RED SILK FROCK

I.

You could not help liking little Annie Conwell; she was so gentle, and had a half shy, half roguish manner, which was very winning. And, then, she was so pretty to look at, with her pink cheeks, soft blue eyes, and light, wavy hair. Though held up as a model child, like most people, including even good little girls, she was fond of her own way; and if she set her heart upon having anything, she wanted it without delay - right then and there. And she usually got it as soon as possible; for Mr. Conwell was one of the kindest of fathers, and if Annie had cried for the moon he would have been distressed because he could not obtain it for her; while, as the two older children, Walter and Josephine, were away at boarding-school, Mrs. Conwell, in her loneliness at their absence, was perhaps more indulgent toward her little daughter than she would otherwise have been.

Annie's great friend was Lucy Caryl. Lucy lived upon the next block; and every day when going to school Annie called for her, or Lucy ran down to see if Annie was ready. Regularly Mrs. Conwell said: "Remember, Annie, I want you to come straight from school, and not stop at the Caryls'. If you want to go and play with Lucy afterward, I have no objection, but you *must* come home first."

"Yes, um," was the docile answer she invariably made.

But, strange as it may seem, although Annie Conwell was considered clever and bright enough in general, and often stood head of her class, she seemed to have a wretched memory in regard to this parting injunction of her mother, or else there were ostensibly many good reasons for making exceptions to the rule. When, as sometimes happened, she entered the house some two hours after school was dismissed, and threw down her books upon the sitting-room table, Mrs. Conwell reproachfully looked up from her sewing and asked: "What time is it, dear?"

And Annie, after a startled glance at the clock, either stammered, "O mother, I forgot!" or else rattled off an unsatisfactory excuse.

"Very well!" was the frequent warning. "If you stay at Lucy Caryl's without permission, you must remain indoors on Saturday as a punishment for your disobedience."

Nevertheless, when the end of the week came, Annie usually managed to escape the threatened penalty. For Saturday is a busy day in the domestic world; and Mrs. Conwell was one of the fine, old-fashioned housekeepers - now, unfortunately, somewhat out of date - who looked well after the ways of her household, which was in consequence pervaded by an atmosphere of comfort and prosperity.

One especial holiday, however, she surprised the little maid by saying,

"Annie, I have told you over and over again that you must come directly home from school, and yet for several days you have not made your appearance until nearly dusk. I am going down town now, and I forbid you to go out to play until I return. For a great girl, going on ten years of age, you are too heedless. Something must be done about it."

Annie reddened, buried her cheeks in the fur of her mother's sable muff with which she was toying, and gave a sidelong glance at Mrs. Conwell's face. The study of it assured her that there was no use in "begging off" this time; so she silently laid down the muff and walked to the window.

Mrs. Conwell, after clasping her handsome fur collar - or tippet, as it was called - over the velvet mantle which was the fashion in those days, and surveying in the mirror the nodding plumes of her bonnet of royal purple hue, took up the muff and went away.

"A great girl!" grumbled Annie, as she watched the lady out of sight. "She always says that when she is displeased. 'Going on ten years of age!' It is true, of course; but, then, I was only nine last month. At other times, when persons ask me how old I am, if I answer 'Most ten,' mother is sure to laugh and say, 'Annie's just past nine.' It makes me so mad!"

There was no use in standing idly thinking about it though, especially as nothing of interest was occurring in the street just then; so Annie turned away and began to wonder what she should do to amuse herself. In the "best china closet" was a delicious cake. She had discovered that the key of the inner cupboard, where it was locked up, was kept in the blue vase on the dining-room mantel. She had been several times "just to take a peep at the cake," she said to herself. Mrs. Conwell had also looked at it occasionally, and it had no appearance of having been interfered with. Yet, somehow, there was a big hole scooped in the middle of it from the under side. The discovery must be made some day, and then matters would not be so pleasant for the meddler; but, in the meantime, this morning Annie concluded to try "just a crumb" of the cake, to make sure it was not getting stale.

Having satisfied herself upon that point, and being at a loss for occupation, she thought she would see what was going on out of doors now. (If some little girls kept account of the minutes they spend in looking out of the window, how astonished they would be at the result!) At present the first person Annie saw was Lucy Caryl, who from the opposite sidewalk was making frantic efforts to attract her attention.

"Come into my house and play with me," Lucy spelled with her fingers in the deaf and dumb alphabet.

Annie raised the sash. "I can't, Lucy!" she called. "Mother said I must stay in the house."

"Oh, do come - just for a little while!" teased naughty Lucy. "Your mother will never know. She has gone away down town: I saw her take the car. We'll watch the corner; when we see her coming, you can run around by the yard and slip in at the gate before she reaches the front door."

The inducement was strong. Annie pretended to herself that she did not understand the uneasy feeling in her heart, which told her she was not doing right. The servants were down in the kitchen, and would not miss her. She ran for her cloak and hood - little girls wore good, warm hoods in those days, - and in a few moments was scurrying along the sidewalk with Lucy.

The Caryls lived in a spacious brown stone house, which exteriorly was precisely like the residence of the Conwells. The interior, however, was very different. Contrasted with the brightness of Annie's home, it presented an appearance of cheerless and somewhat dingy grandeur. The parlors, now seldom used, were furnished in snuff-colored damask, a trifle faded; the curtains, of the same heavy material, had a stuffy look, and made one long to throw open the window to get a breath of fresh air. The walls were adorned with remarkable tapestries in great gilt frames, testimonials to the industry of Mrs. Caryl during her girlhood. Here and there, too, hung elaborate souvenirs of departed members of the family, in the shape of memorial crosses and wreaths of waxed flowers, also massively framed. They were very imposing; but Annie had a nervous horror of them, and invariably hurried past that parlor door.

The little girls usually played together in a small room adjoining the sitting-room. They had by no means the run of the house. Annie, indeed, felt a certain awe of Lucy's mother, who was stern and severe with children.

"I'm sure I shouldn't care to go to the Caryls', except that Lucy is so seldom allowed to come to see me," she often declared.

On this particular afternoon Mrs. Caryl had also gone out.

"My Aunt Mollie sent me some lovely clothes for my doll," said Lucy. "The box is up on the top story. Come with me to get it."

Remembering the "funeral flowers," as Annie called them, she had an idea that Lucy's mother kept similar or even more uncanny treasures stored away "on the top story," which her imagination invested with an air of mystery. So she hesitated.

"Come!" repeated Lucy, who forthwith tripped on ahead, and looked over the baluster to see why she did not follow.

Annie hesitated no longer, but started up the steps. Just at that moment a peculiar sound, like the clanging of a chain, followed by a strange, rustling noise, came from one of the rooms above. A foolish terror seized upon her.

"O gracious! what's that?" she panted; and, turning, would have fled down the stairs again, had not Lucy sprung toward her and caught her dress.

"It's nothing, goosie!" said she, "except Jim. He's been a naughty boy, and is tied up in the front room. Ma thought she'd try that plan so he could not slip out to go skating. I suppose I ought to have told you, though. Maybe you thought we had a crazy person up here."

Annie forced herself to laugh. Reassured in a measure, and still more curious, she ventured to go on. When she reached the upper hall, she saw that the door of the front room was open, and, looking in, beheld a comical spectacle. Fastened by a stout rope to one of the high posts of an old-fashioned bedstead was a rollicking urchin of about eight years of age, who seemed to be having a very good time, notwithstanding his captivity. Upon his shoes were a pair of iron clamps resembling spurs, such as were used for skates. It was the clank of these against the brass balls, of which there was one at the top of each post, which made the sound that had so frightened Annie.

"Hello!" he called out as he caught sight of her. And, fascinated by the novelty of the situation, she stood a moment watching his antics, which were similar to those of a monkey upon a pole. Again and again he climbed the post, indulged in various acrobatic performances upon the foot-board, and then turned a double somersault right into the centre of the great feather-bed. And all the while his villainous little iron-bound heels made woful work, leaving countless dents and scratches upon the fine old mahogany, and catching in the meshes of the handsome knitted counterpane.

"You'd better stop that!" Lucy called to him.

In response to her advice, he clambered over and seated himself upon the mantel.

"Oh! oh!" she expostulated in alarm, lest the shelf should fall beneath his weight.

As that catastrophe did not occur, he coolly shifted his position, made a teasing grimace at her, and when she turned away slipped down and resumed his gymnastic exercises.

There was nothing else on the top story to excite Annie's surprise, but she was glad when Lucy secured the box and led the way downstairs.

II.

"When the little friends were again in their accustomed play corner, Lucy, with much satisfaction, displayed her present.

"Your Aunt Mollie must be awful nice!" exclaimed Annie. "How lucky you are! Three more dresses for your doll! Clementina has not had any new clothes for a long time. I think that red silk dress is the prettiest, don't you?"

"I haven't quite decided," answered Lucy. "Christabel looks lovely in it; but I think the blue one is perhaps even more becoming."

They tried the various costumes upon Lucy's doll, and admired the effect of each in turn.

"Still, I like the red silk dress best," said Annie.

"It would just suit Clementina, wouldn't it?" suggested Lucy.

"Yes," sighed Annie, taking up the little frock, and imagining she saw her own doll attired in its gorgeousness. After regarding it enviously for a few moments, she said: "Say, Lucy, give it to me, won't you?"

"Why, the idea!" cried Lucy, aghast at the audacity of the proposal.

"I think you might," pouted Annie. "You hardly ever give me anything, although you are my dearest friend. I made you a present of Clementina's second best hat for Christabel, and only yesterday I gave you that sweet bead ring you asked me for."

These unanswerable arguments were lost upon Lucy, however. She snatched away the tiny frock, and both little girls sulked a while.

"Lucy's real mean!" said Annie to herself. "She ought to give it to me, - she knows she ought! Oh, dear, I want it awfully! She owes me something for what I've given her. - I am going home," she announced aloud.

"Oh, no!" protested Lucy, aroused to the sense of her duties as hostess. "Let us put away the dolls and read. There is a splendid new story this week in the *Young Folks' Magazine*."

Taking Annie's silence for assent, she packed Christabel and her belongings away again, and went to get the book. Annie waited sullenly. Then, as her friend did not come back immediately, she began to fidget.

"Lucy need not have been in such a hurry to whisk her things into the box," she complained. "To look at the red dress won't spoil it, I suppose. I *will* have another look at it, anyhow!"

She raised the cover of the box and took out the dainty dress. Still Lucy did not return. A temptation came to Annie. Why not keep the pretty red silk frock? Lucy would not miss it at once; afterward she would think she had mislaid it. She would never suspect the truth. Annie breathed hard. If she had quickly put the showy bit of trumpery back into the box and banished the covetous wish, all would have been well; but instead, she stood deliberating and turning the little dress over and over in her hands. Meantime a hospitable thought had occurred to Lucy. She remembered that there was a new supply of apples in the pantry, and had gone to get one for Annie and one for herself. On her way through the dining-room she happened to look out of the window.

"Goodness gracious!" she exclaimed; for there was Mrs. Conwell getting out of the car at the corner!

At Lucy's call of, "Annie, here comes your mother!" Annie started, hesitated, glanced at the box, and, alas! crammed the red silk frock into her pocket. Then she caught up her cloak and hood, and rushed down the stairs. Lucy ran to open the yard gate for her, and thrust the apple into her hand as she passed.

Flurried and short of breath, she reached home just as Mrs. Conwell rang the door-bell. She did not hasten as usual to greet her mother; but, hurrying to her own little room, shut herself in, and sat down on the bed to recover from her confusion.

It happened that the cook claimed Mrs. Conwell's attention in regard to some domestic matter, and thus she did not at once inquire for her little daughter, supposing that the child was contentedly occupied. Annie, therefore, had some time in which to collect her thoughts. As her excitement gradually died away, she found that, instead of feeling the satisfaction she expected in having spent the afternoon as she pleased and yet escaped discovery, she was restless and unhappy. Upon her neat dressing-table lay the apple which Lucy had given her. It was ripe and rosy, but she felt that a bite of it would choke her. Above the head of the bed hung a picture of the Madonna with the Divine Child. Obeying a sudden impulse, she jumped up and turned it inward to the wall. Ah, Annie, what a coward a guilty conscience can make of the bravest among us!

Glancing cautiously around, as if the very walls had eyes and could reveal what they saw, she drew from her pocket the red silk frock. She sat and gazed at it as if in a dream. It was as pretty as ever, yet it no longer gave her pleasure. She did not dare to try it on Clementina; she wanted to hide it away in some corner where no one would ever find it. Tiny as it was, she felt that it could never be successfully concealed; Remorse would point it out wherever it was secreted. Annie began to realize what she had done. She had stolen! She, proud Annie Conwell, who held her head so high, whom half the girls at school envied, had taken what did not belong to her! How her cheeks burned! She wondered if it had been found out yet. What would Lucy say? Would she tell all the girls, and would they avoid her, and whisper together when she was around, saying, "Look out for Annie Conwell! She is not to be trusted."

She covered her face with her hands, and burst into tears. And all the while a low voice kept whispering in her heart with relentless persistency, till human respect gave way to higher motives. She glanced up at the picture, turned it around again with a feeling of compunction, and, humbled and contrite, sank on her knees in a little heap upon the floor.

A few moments afterward her mother's step sounded in the hall. When one finds a little girl's cloak flung on the baluster, stumbles over a hood on the stairs, and picks up an odd mitten somewhere else, the evidences are strong that the owner has come home in a hurry. Mrs. Conwell had, therefore, discovered Annie's disobedience. She threw open the door, intending to rebuke her severely; but the sight of the child's flushed and tear-stained face checked the chiding words upon her lips.

"What is the matter, Annie?" she inquired, somewhat sternly.

"O mother, please don't scold me! I'm unhappy enough already," faltered Annie, beginning to cry again.

Then, as the burden of her miserable little secret had become unendurable, she told the whole story. Mrs. Conwell looked pained and grave, but her manner was very gentle as she said:

"Of course, the first thing for you to do is to return what you have unjustly taken."

Annie gave a little nervous shudder. "What! go and tell Lucy I stole her doll's red silk dress?" she exclaimed. "How could I ever!"

"I do not say it is necessary to do that," answered her mother; "but you are certainly obliged to restore it. I should advise you to take it back without delay, and have the struggle over."

She went away, and left the little girl to reflect upon the matter. But the more Annie debated with herself, the more difficulty she had in coming to a decision. Finally she started up, exclaiming,

"The longer I think about it the harder it seems. I'll just *do it* right off."

She picked up the dress, darted down the stairs, hurriedly prepared to go out, and in a few moments was hastening down the block to the Caryls'. Lucy saw her coming, and met her at the door.

"Did you get a scolding? Was your mother very much displeased?" she asked; for she perceived immediately that Annie had been crying, and misinterpreted the cause of her tears.

"Oh, no! - well, I suppose she was," hesitated Annie. "But she did not say much."

"How did she happen to let you come down here again?" continued Lucy, leading the way to the sitting-room.

Annie cast a quick glance at the table. The box which contained Christabel and her wardrobe was no longer there. It was useless, then, to hope for a chance to quietly slip the red dress into it again.

Lucy repeated the question, wondering what had set her playmate's thoughts a-wool-gathering.

"I'm not going to stay," began Annie.

Lucy's clear eyes met hers inquiringly. To her uneasy conscience they seemed to accuse her and to demand the admission of her fault. Her cheeks grew crimson; and, as a person in a burning building ventures a perilous leap in the hope of escape, so Annie, finding her present position intolerable, stammered out the truth.

"I only came to bring back something. Don't be vexed, will you, at what I'm going to tell you? I took that red silk dress home with me; but here it is, and I'm sorry, Lucy, - indeed I am!"

A variety of expressions flitted across Lucy's face as she listened. Incredulity, surprise, and indignation were depicted there. Annie had stated the case as mildly as possible, but Lucy understood. After the first surprise, however, she began to comprehend dimly that it must have required a good deal of moral courage thus openly to bring back the little dress. She was conscious of a new respect for Annie, who stood there so abashed. For a few moments there was an awkward pause; then she managed to say:

"Oh, that is all right! Of course I should have been vexed if you had not brought it back, because I should have missed it as soon as I opened the box. I was mean about it, anyway. I might have let you take it to try on Clementina. Here, I'll give it to you now, to make up for being stingy."

Annie shook her head, and refused to take the once coveted gift from her companion's outstretched hand.

"Then I'll lend it to you for ever and ever," continued Lucy, impulsively.

"No, I don't want it now," answered Annie. "Good-bye!"

"Will you go to walk with me to-morrow after Sunday-school?" urged Lucy, as she followed her to the door.

"P'rhaps!" replied her little friend, hastening away.

The inquiry brought her a feeling of relief, however. Lucy evidently had no thought of "cutting" her acquaintance. The sense of having done right made her heart light and happy as she ran home. The experience had taught her that one must learn to see many pretty things without wishing to possess them; and also that small acts of disobedience and a habit of meddling may lead further than one at first intends.

Annie became a lovely woman, a devoted daughter, a most self-sacrificing character, and one scrupulously exact in her dealings with others; but she never forgot "that red silk frock."

"A LESSON WITH A SEQUEL"

"How strange that any one should be so superstitious!" said Emily Mahon. Rosemary Beckett had been telling a group of girls of the ridiculous practices of an old negro woman employed by her mother as a laundress.

"People must be very ignorant to believe such things," declared Anna Shaw, disdainfully.

"Yet," observed Miss Graham, closing the new magazine which she had been looking over, "it is surprising how many persons, who ought to know better, are addicted to certain superstitions, and cannot be made to see that it is not only foolish but wrong to yield to them."

"Well," began Rosemary, "I am happy to say that is not a failing of mine."

"I think everything of the kind is nonsensical," added Kate Parsons.

"I'm not a bit superstitious either," volunteered Emily.

"Nor I," interposed Anna.

"I despise such absurdities," continued May Johnston.

"My dear girls," laughed Miss Graham, "I'll venture to say that each one of you has a pet superstition, which influences you more or less, and which you ought to overcome."

This assertion was met by a chorus of indignant protests.

"Why, Cousin Irene!" cried Emily.

"O, Miss Graham, how *can* you think so!"

"The very idea!" etc., etc., chimed in the others.

Everybody liked Miss Irene Graham. She lived with her cousins, the Mahons, and supported herself by giving lessons to young girls who for various reasons did not attend a regular school. Her classes were popular, not only because she was bright and clever, and had the faculty of imparting what she knew; but because, as parents soon discovered, she taught her pupils good, sound common-sense, as well as "the shallower knowledge of books." Cousin Irene had not forgotten how she used to think and feel when she herself was a young girl, and therefore she was able to look at the world from a girl's point of view, to sympathize with her dreams and undertakings. She did not look for very wise heads upon young shoulders; but when she found that her pupils had foolish notions, or did not behave sensibly, she tried to make them see this for themselves; and we all know from experience that what we learn in that way produces the most lasting impression.

The girls now gathered around her were members of the literature class, which met on Wednesday and Saturday mornings at the Mahons'. As they considered themselves accomplished and highly cultivated for their years, it was mortifying to be accused of being so unenlightened as to believe in omens.

"No, I haven't a particle of superstition," repeated Rosemary, decidedly. "There's one thing I won't do, though. I won't give or accept a present of anything sharp - a knife or scissors, or even a pin, - because, the saying is, it cuts friendship. I've found it so, too. I gave Clara Hayes a silver hair-pin at Christmas, and a few weeks after we quarrelled."

"There is the fault, popping up like a Jack-in-the box!" said Miss Irene. "But, if I remember, Clara was a new acquaintance of yours in the holidays, and you and she were inseparable. The ardor of such extravagant friendship soon cools. Before long you concluded you did not like her so well as at first; then came the disagreement. But is it not silly to say the pin had anything to do with the matter? Would it not have been the same if you had given her a book or a picture?"

"If I'm walking in the street with a friend, I'm always careful never to let any person or thing come between us," admitted Kate Parsons. "It's a sure sign that you'll be disappointed -"

"Oh, it will be all right if you remember to say 'Bread and butter!'" interrupted Anna, eagerly.

They all laughed; but Miss Irene saw by the tell-tale faces of several that they clung to this childish practice.

"We used to do so in play when we were little girls," said Emily, apologetically; "and I suppose it became a habit."

"The other day," Miss Graham went on, "I heard a young lady say: 'If you are setting out upon a journey, or even a walk, and have to go back to the house for anything, be sure you sit down before starting off again.' It is bad luck not to do so.'"

Emily colored.

"Yes, we are very particular about that!" cried Rosemary, impulsively, as her companions did not contradict the avowal; it was evident that she knew what she was talking about.

The conversation turned to other subjects. Presently Anna and Rosemary were planning an excursion to a neighboring town.

"To visit Elizabeth Harris, who was at the convent with us last year," explained the latter. "Suppose we go to-morrow?"

"I have an engagement with the dentist," was the doleful reply.

"Well, the day after?"

"Let me see," mused Anna. "Oh, no!" she added, hastily. "I could not start on a journey or begin any work on a Friday; it would not be lucky, you know!" Then she flushed and looked toward Miss Irene, who shook her head significantly and wrote in her note-book, "Superstitious practice No. 4."

As it was Emily's birthday, the girls had been invited to stay for luncheon. Emily now led the way to the dining-room, where a pretty table was spread. Everything was as dainty as good taste and handsome auxiliaries could make it: the snowy damask, fine glass, and old family silver; the small crystal bowls filled with chrysanthemums, and at each plate a tiny bouquet.

Mr. Mahon was down town at his business, but there stood Mrs. Mahon, so kind and affable; and the boys and girls of the family were waiting to take their seats. The party paused, while, according to the good old-fashioned custom (now too often neglected), grace was said; and Cousin Irene, contemplating the bright faces and pleasant surroundings, thought she had seldom seen a more attractive picture. But now she noticed that May, after a quick look around, appeared startled and anxious. The next moment the foolish girl exclaimed:

"O Mrs. Mahon, there are thirteen of us here! You do not like to have thirteen persons at your table, do you? Pardon me, but I'm so nervous about it!"

A shadow of annoyance flitted across Mrs. Mahon's motherly countenance, but she answered gently: "My dear, I never pay any attention to the superstition. Still a hostess will not insist upon making a guest uncomfortable. Tom," she continued, addressing her youngest son, "you will oblige me by taking your luncheon afterward."

Tom scowled at May, flung himself out of his chair, mumbled

something about "stuff and nonsense;" and, avoiding his mother's reproving glance, went off in no amiable humor.

May was embarrassed, especially as she felt Miss Irene's grave eyes fixed upon her. But Mrs. Mahon was too courteous to allow any one to remain disconcerted at her hospitable board. With ready tact she managed that the little incident should seem speedily forgotten. After a momentary awkwardness the girls began to chatter merrily again, and harmony was restored.

On their return to the drawing-room, May whispered to Miss Graham: "I hope Mrs. Mahon will excuse me for calling her attention to the number at table. I did not mean to be rude, and I suppose it is silly to be so superstitious; but, indeed, I can not help it."

"Do not say that, dear; because you can help it if you wish," was the gentle reply, "Mrs. Mahon understood, I am sure, that you did not intend to be impolite; but I know she must have felt regret that you should give way to such folly." Then, turning to the others, Miss Irene continued: "Well, girls, considering the revelations of this morning, perhaps you will admit that you have, after all, a fair share of superstition."

"I'm afraid so," acknowledged Rosemary; and no one demurred.

"Do you know how these superstitions originated, Miss Graham?" asked Anna, who was of an inquiring mind.

"Many of them are very ancient," replied Cousin Irene. "That which predicts that the gift of anything sharp cuts friendship probably dates back farther than the days of Rome and Greece, and is almost as old as the dagger itself. No doubt it originated in an age of frequent wars and quarrels, when for a warrior to put a weapon in the hands of a companion was perhaps to find it forthwith turned against himself. In those days of strife also, when men were more ready in action than in the turning of phrases, and so much was expressed by symbolism, the offering of a sword or dagger was frequently in itself a challenge, and a declaration of enmity. Thus, you see, that what was a natural inference in other times is meaningless in ours. The adage which advises the person obliged to turn back in his journey to be careful to sit down before setting out anew, was at first simply a metaphorical way of saying that having made a false start toward the accomplishment of any duty, it is well to begin again at the beginning. The custom which restrained comrades in arms, or friends walking or journeying together, from allowing anything to come between them, had also a figurative import. It was a dramatic manner of declaring, 'Nothing shall ever part us, - no ill-will nor strife, not even this accidental barrier, shall interrupt our friendly intercourse.' In the times, too, when there were few laws but that of might, when danger often lurked by the wayside, it was always well for a traveller to keep close to his companion, and not to separate from him without necessity.

"Many other superstitions, as well, have a symbolical origin. But the nineteenth century does not deal with such picturesque methods of expression. We pride ourselves upon saying in so many words just what we mean; therefore much of the poetic imagery of other days has no significance in ours. And is it not symbolism without sense which constitutes one of the phases of superstition? As for your bread-and-butter exorcism, Anna, I presume it was simply the expression of a hope that nothing might interfere between hungry folk and their dinner. This is, indeed, but a bit of juvenile nonsense; just as children will 'make believe' that some dire mishap will befall one who steps on the cracks of a flagged sidewalk; and so on through a score of funny conceits and games, innocent enough as child's play, but hardly worthy of sensible girls in their teens.

"You know, the practice of refraining from beginning a journey or undertaking on Friday," continued Miss Irene, "arose from a religious observance of the day upon which Our Lord was crucified. As the early Christians were accustomed to devote this day to meditation and prayer, it followed that few went abroad at that time, or set about new temporal ventures. Superstition early perverted the import of this pious custom. As on that day Satan marshalled all the powers of evil against the Son of God, so, said the soothsayers, he would beset with misfortune and danger the path of those who set forth on a Friday. As regards the case in point, since we do not go into retreat once a week, I presume Anna and Rosemary have not this reason for refusing to visit their young friend on Friday."

There was a general laugh, after which Miss Irene went on:

"For the rest, we know God's loving providence carefully watches over us at all times, and constantly preserves us from countless dangers; that nothing can betide us without His permission, and that He blesses the work of every day if we ask Him. Far from being influenced by the common superstition with regard to Friday, it would seem as if we should piously prefer to begin an undertaking (and in this spirit seek a special blessing on the work thus commenced) on the day of the week which commemorates that most fortunate of all days for us, on which was consummated the great act of Redemption.

"The superstition with reference to thirteen at table dates from the Last Supper, of which Our Lord partook with His twelve Apostles on the eve of His crucifixion. Hence the saying that of thirteen persons who sit down together to a repast, one will soon die. I think it was originally the custom to avoid having thirteen at the festive or family board, not so much from this notion, as to express a horror of the treachery of Judas. Such would be, for instance, the chivalrous spirit of the Crusaders. We can understand how, in feudal times, a knight would consider it an affront to his fellows to bid them to a banquet spread for thirteen. In those days, when a feast was so apt to end in a fray, - when by perfidy the enemy so often entered at the castle gate while the company were at table, and frequently a chief was slain ere he could rise from his place, - the circumstance would point an analogy which it has not with us, suggesting not merely mortality but betrayal; a breach of all the laws of hospitality; impending death by violence. Since we can not live forever, among every assemblage of individuals there is likely to be one at least whose life may be nearly at its close. The more persons present, the greater the probability; therefore there is really a greater fatality in the numbers fourteen, twenty, thirty, than in thirteen.

"But to return to the point from which we started - no, Emily, it is not necessary to sit down. You will observe that many persons who declare emphatically that they are not superstitious, are nevertheless influenced by old-time sayings and practices; some of which, though perhaps beautiful originally, have now lost all significance; others which are simply relics of paganism. Men are often as irrational in this respect as women; and, notice this well, you will find superstition much more common among non-Catholics than among Catholics. As we have seen, however, some of us do not realize that what we are pleased to call certain harmless eccentricities, are very like the superstitious practices forbidden by the First Commandment."

Kate and Emily were not giving to this little homily the attention it deserved. They had begun to trifle as girls are wont to do. Catching at the tiny bisque cupid that hung from the chandelier, Emily sportively sent it flying toward Kate, who swung it back again. Thus they kept it flitting to and fro, faster and faster. Finally, Emily hit it with a jerk. The cord by which it was suspended snapped; the dainty bit of bric-a-brac sped across the room, and, striking with full force against a mirror in a quaint old secretary that had belonged to Mr. Mahon's uncle, shivered the glass to pieces. Instantly every trace of color fled from her face, and she stood appalled, gazing at the mischief she had done. There was, of course, an exclamation from her companions, who remained staring at her, and appeared almost as disturbed as herself.

Cousin Irene went over and patted her on the shoulder, saying, "Do not be so distressed, child. I know you are sorry to have damaged the old secretary, which we value so much for its associations. But there is no need of being so troubled. We can have a new mirror put in."

"It is not only that," faltered the silly girl; "but to break a looking-glass! You know it is a sure sign that a great misfortune will befall us - that there will probably be a death in the family before long."

"Oh, but such sayings don't always come true! There are often exceptions," interposed Kate, anxious to say something consolatory, and heartily wishing they had let the little cupid alone.

"Too bad; for it really is dreadfully unlucky to have such a thing happen!" sighed Rosemary, with less tact.

"I know it," murmured May.

"Yes, indeed," added Anna.

Miss Graham drew back astonished. "Young ladies, I am ashamed of you!" she said, reproachfully, and went out of the room.

There were a few moments of discomfiture, and presently the girls concluded, one after another, that it was time to be going home.

Left alone, Emily approached the secretary and examined the ruined mirror. It was cracked like an egg-shell, - "smashed to smithereens," Tom said in telling the story later; but only one or two bits had fallen out. Idly attempting to fit these into place again, Emily caught sight of what she supposed was a sheet of note-paper, that had apparently made its way in between the back of the mirror and the frame.

"An old letter of grandpa's, probably," she said aloud, taking hold of the corner to draw it out. It stuck fast; but a second effort released it, amid a shower of splintered glass; and to her amazement she found in her possession a time-stained document that had a mysteriously legal air. Trembling with excitement she unfolded it, and, without stopping to think

MARY CATHERINE CROWLEY

that it might not be for her eyes, began to read the queer writing, which was somewhat difficult to decipher:

"In the name of the Father, and of the Son, and of the Holy Ghost. Amen. I, Bernard Mahon, being of sound and disposing mind, do hereby declare this to be my last will and testament."

"Uncle Bernard's will!" gasped Emily. "It must be the one father always said uncle told him about, but which never could be found. Perhaps he slipped it in here for safe-keeping." Eagerly she scanned it, crying at last, "Yes, yes! Hurrah! O Cousin Irene!" she called out, hearing the latter's step in the hall.

When Miss Graham entered Emily was waltzing around the room, waving the document ecstatically. "See what I've found!" she cried, darting toward her with an impulsive caress.

Cousin Irene took the paper, and, as she perused it, became, though in a less demonstrative fashion, as agitated as Emily. "Your father!" she stammered.

Mr. Mahon had come into the house and was now in the little study, which he called his den. Cousin Irene and Emily almost flew thither, and a few minutes later his voice, with a glad ring in it, was heard calling first his wife and then the children to tell them the joyful news.

The will so long sought, so strangely brought to light, made a great change in the family fortunes. By it Bryan, the old man's son, who was unmarried and dissipated, was entitled to merely a certain income and life-interest in the estate, which upon his demise was to go to the testator's nephew William (Mr. Mahon) and Cousin Irene. In fact, however, at his father's death, Bryan, as no will was discovered, had entered into full possession of the property; and when within a year his own career was suddenly cut short, it was learned that he had bequeathed nothing to his relatives but a few family heirlooms.

"I did not grudge Bryan what he had while he lived," said Mr. Mahon; "but when, after the poor fellow was drowned, we heard that he had left all his money to found a library for 'the Preservation of the Records of Sport and Sportsmen,' I did feel that, with my boys and girls to provide for and educate, I could have made a better use of it. And Cousin Irene would have been saved a good deal of hard work if she could have obtained her share at the time. Thank God it is all right now, and the library with the long name will have to wait for another founder."

The girls of the literature class soon heard of their friends' good fortune, and were not slow in offering their congratulations.

One day, some two years after, when Anna and Rosemary happened to call at the Mahons', a chance reference was made to the discovery of the will. "Only think," exclaimed Rosemary, "how much came about through the spoiling of that mirror! Emily, you surely can never again believe it unlucky to break a looking-glass?"

"No, indeed!" replied Emily, thinking of the uninterrupted happiness and prosperity which the family had enjoyed since then.

"It was a fortunate accident for us," said Cousin Irene; "but I should not advise any one to go around smashing all the looking-glasses in his or her house, hoping for a similar result. It certainly would be an unlucky sign for the person who had to meet the bill for repairs."

"Miss Graham, how do you suppose this superstition originated?" asked Anna, as eager for information as ever. After a general laugh at her expense, Cousin Irene said:

"The first mirrors, you must remember, were the forest pools and mountain tarns. As the hunter stooped to one of these to slake his thirst, if perchance so much as a shadow should break

MARY CATHERINE CROWLEY

the reflection of his own image in its tranquil depths, he had reason to fear that danger and perhaps death were at hand; for often in some such dark mirror a victim caught the first glimpse of his enemy, who had been waiting in ambush and was now stealing upon him from behind; or of the wild beast making ready to leap upon him. But the popular augury that the mere fact of breaking a looking-glass portends death, is, you must see, senseless and absurd. And so, as I think you have become convinced, are all superstitions. It is true we sometimes remark coincidences, and are inclined to make much of them; without noting, on the contrary, how many times the same supposed omens and signs come to nought. When God wills to send us some special happiness or trial, be assured He makes use of no such means to prepare us for it; since He directs our lives not by chance, but by His all-wise and loving Providence."

UNCLE TOM'S STORY

I.

Some pine logs burned brightly upon the andirons in the wide, old-fashioned chimney; and the Tyrrell children were comfortably seated around the fire, roasting chestnuts and telling stories.

"Come, Uncle Tom, it is your turn!" cried Pollie, breaking in upon the reverie of their mother's brother, who, seated in the old red arm-chair, was gazing abstractedly at the cheery flames.

"Yes, please let us have something about the war," put in Rob.

"But everybody has been telling war stories for the last twenty-five years. Do you not think we have had enough of them?" said the gentleman.

"One never tires of hearing of deeds of bravery," answered Rob, dramatically.

"Or of romantic adventures," added Pollie.

Uncle Tom looked amused; but, after some hesitation, said; "Well, I will tell you an incident recalled by this pine-wood fire. It may seem extraordinary; but, having witnessed it myself, I can vouch for its truth. You consider me an old soldier; yet, though I wore the blue uniform for more than a year and saw some fighting, I was only a youth of eighteen when the war closed; and, in spite of my boyish anxiety to distinguish myself and become a hero, I probably would never

MARY CATHERINE CROWLEY

have attained even to the rank of orderly, had it not come about in the following manner:"

Our regiment was stationed at A ---, not far from the seat of war. Near our quarters was a Catholic church, attended by the --- Fathers. I early made the acquaintance of one of them, who was popularly known as Father *Friday*, this being the nearest approach to the pronunciation of his peculiar German name to which the majority of the people could arrive. In him I recognized my ideal of a Christian gentleman, and as such I still revere his memory.

He was one of the handsomest men I ever saw - tall and of splendid physique, with light brown hair, blue eyes, and a complexion naturally fair, but bronzed by the sun. Though in reality he was as humble and unassuming as any lay-brother in his community, his bearing was simply regal.

He could not have helped it any more than he could help the impress of nobility upon his fine features. The youngsters used to enjoy seeing him pass the contribution box in church at special collections. It must have been "an act" (as you convent girls say, Pollie). He would move along in his superb manner, looking right over the heads of the congregation, and disdaining to cast a glance at the "filthy lucre" that was being heaped up in the box which from obedience he carried. What were silver and gold, let alone the cheap paper currency of the times, to him, who had given up wealth and princely rank to become a religious! Yet, in fact, they were a great deal, since they meant help for the needy - a church built, a hospital for the sick poor. In this sense none appreciated more the value of money.

Father Friday was accustomed to travel about the country for miles, hunting up those of his flock who, from the unsettled state of affairs, either could not or would not come into the town to church. Like the typical missionary, from necessity he always walked; though, in my youthful enthusiasm, I used to think how grandly he would look upon a charger and in the uniform of a general. In his old cassock, and wearing a hat either of plain brown straw or black felt, according to the season, he was as intrepid as a general, however; and went about alone as serenely as if the times were most peaceful. Our colonel often remonstrated with him for doing so, and finally insisted upon appointing an orderly to attend him. Father Friday at first declined; but upon hearing that the duty had been assigned to me, he in the end assented - partly, I suppose, to keep me from bad company and out of mischief. Many a pleasant tramp I had with him; for he would beguile the way with anecdotes and jokes, and bits of information upon geology, botany, the birds of that section - everything likely to interest a boy. What wonder that I regarded a day with him as a genuine holiday?

One October afternoon he said: "To-morrow morning, Captain Tom" (the title was a pleasantry of his), - "to-morrow morning I shall be glad of your company. I am going some five miles back into the country to visit an invalid."

"Very well, Father," I answered. "I shall be ready."

Accordingly, the next day, at the appointed hour, I joined him at the gate of the convent, and we set out - this time in silence, for he carried the Blessed Sacrament. At first our course was through the open plain; but later it led, for perhaps a mile, across a corner of the pine forest, which extended all along the ridge and shut the valley in from the rest of the world. We entered the wood confidently, and for half an hour followed the windings of the path, which gradually became less defined. After a while it began to appear that we were making but little headway.

Father Friday stopped. "Does it not seem to you that we are merely going round and round, Tom?" he asked.

I assented gloomily.

"Have you a compass?"

MARY CATHERINE CROWLEY

I shook my head.

"Nor have I," he added. "I did not think of bringing one, being so sure of the way. How could we have turned from it so inadvertently? Well, we must calculate by the sun. The point for which we are bound is in a southerly direction."

Having taken our bearings, we retraced our steps a short distance, then pushed forward for an hour or more, without coming out upon the bridle-path which we expected to find. Another hour passed; the sun was getting high. Father Friday paused again.

"What time is it?" he inquired.

I looked at the little silver watch my mother gave me when I left home. "Nine o'clock!" I answered, with a start.

"How unfortunate!" he exclaimed. "There is now no use in pressing on farther. We should arrive too late at our destination. We may as well rest a little, and then try to find our way home. It is unaccountable that I should have missed the way so stupidly."

But it was one thing to order a retreat, as we soldiers would call it, and quite another to go back by the route we had come. We followed first one track and then another; but the under-brush grew thicker and thicker, and at length the conviction was forced upon us that we were completely astray. I climbed a tree - it was no easy task, as any one who has ever attempted to climb a pine will agree. I got up some distance, after a fashion; but the branches were so thick and the trees so close together that there was nothing to be discerned, except that I was surrounded by what seemed miles of green boughs, which swayed in the breeze, making me think of the waves of an emerald sea.

I scrambled down and submitted my discouraging report. The sun was now overhead: it must therefore be noon. We began to feel that even a frugal meal would be welcome. I had managed to get a cup of coffee before leaving my quarters; but Father Friday, I suspected, had taken nothing. We succeeded in finding some berries here and there; and, farther on, a spring of water. However, this primitive fare was of little avail to satisfy one's appetite.

Well, after wandering about, and shouting and hallooing till we were tired, in the effort to attract the attention of any one who might chance to be in the vicinity, we rested at the foot of a tree. Father Friday recited some prayers, to which I made the responses. Then he withdrew a little, and read his Office as serenely as if he were in the garden of the convent; while I, weary and disheartened, threw myself on the ground and tried again to determine by the sun where we were. I must have fallen asleep; for the next thing I knew the sun was considerably lower, and Father Friday was waiting to make another start.

"How strange," he kept repeating as we proceeded, "that we should be so entirely astray in a wood only a few miles in extent, and within such a short distance from home! It is most extraordinary. I cannot understand it."

It was, indeed, singular; but I was too dispirited to speculate upon the subject. Soldier though I prided myself upon being, and strong, active fellow that I certainly was, Father Friday was as far ahead of me in his endurance of the hardship of our position as in everything else.

Dusk came, and we began to fear that we should have to remain where we were all night. Again I climbed a tree, hoping to catch a glimpse of a light somewhere. All was dark, however; and I was about to descend when - surely there was a faint glimmer yonder! As the diver peers amid the depths of the sea in search of buried jewels, so I eagerly looked down among the green branches. Yes, now it became a ray, and probably shone from some dwelling in the heart of the wood. I called the good news to Father Friday.

"*Deo gratias!*" he exclaimed. "Where is it?"

"Over there," said I, pointing in the direction of the light.

I got to the ground as fast as I could, and we made our way toward it. Soon we saw it plainly, glowing among the trees; and, following its guidance, soon came to a cleared space, where stood a rude log cabin, in front of which burned a fire of pine knots. Before it was a man of the class which the darkies were wont to designate as "pore white trash." He was a tall, gawky countryman, rawboned, with long, unkempt hair. His homespun clothes were decidedly the worse for wear; his trousers were tucked into the tops of his heavy cowhide boots, and perched upon his head was the roughest of home-woven straw-hats.

At the sound of our footsteps he turned, and to say that he was surprised at our appearance would but ill describe his amazement. Father Friday speedily assured him that we were neither raiders nor bush-rangers, but simply two very hungry wanderers who had been astray in the woods all day.

"Wa-all now, strangers, them is raither hard lines," said the man, good-naturedly. "Jest make yerselves ter home hyere ternight, an' in the mornin' I'll put yer on the right road to A ---. Lors, but yer must a-had a march! Been purty much all over the woods, I reckon. - Mirandy!" he continued, calling to some one inside the cabin. "Mirandy!"

"I'm a-heedin', Josh. What's the matter?" inquired a *scrawny*, sandy-haired woman, coming to the door, with her arms akimbo. "Mussy me!" she ejaculated upon seeing us.

"Hyere's two folks as has got lost in this hyere forest, an' is plum tired out an' powerful hongry," explained her husband.
"Mussy me!" she repeated, eyeing my blue coat askance, and regarding Father Friday with suspicious wonder. She had never seen a uniform like that long black cassock. To which side did he belong, Federal or Confederate?

"Mirandy's Secesh, but I'm for the Union," explained Josh, with a wink to us. "Sometimes we have as big a war as any one cyares ter see, right hyere, on 'ccount of it. But, Lors, Mirandy, yer ain't a-goin' ter quarrel with a man 'cause the color of his coat ain't ter yer likin' when he ain't had a bite of vittles terday!"

"No, I ain't," answered the woman, stolidly. Glancing again at Father Friday's kind face, she added, more graciously: "Wa-all, yer jest in the nick of time; the hoe-cake's nyearly done, and we war about havin' supper. Hey, Josh?"

"Sartain sure," said Josh, ushering us into the kitchen, which was the principal room of the cabin, though a door at the side apparently led into a smaller one adjoining. He made us sit down at the table, and Mirandy placed the best her simple larder afforded before us.

As we went out by the fire again, our host said, with some embarrassment: "Now, strangers, I know ye're fagged out, an' for sure ye're welcome to the tiptop of everythin' we've got. But I'm blessed if I can tell whar ye're a-goin' ter sleep ternight. We've company, yer see, in the leetle room yonder; an' that's the only place we've got ter offer, ordinar'ly."

Father Friday hastened to reassure him. "I propose to establish myself outside by the fire. What could be better?" said he.

Father Friday, you remember, had the Blessed Sacrament with him; and I knew that, weary as he was, he would pass the night in prayer.

"I am actually too tired to sleep now," I began. "But when I am inclined to do so, what pleasanter resting-place could a soldier desire than a bit of ground strewn with pine needles?"

"Wa-all, I allow I'm glad yer take it the right way," declared Josh; then, growing loquacious, he continued: "Fact is, this is mighty cur'ous company of ourn -"

"Josh, come hyere a minute, can't yer?" called Mirandy from within.

"Sartain," he answered, breaking off abruptly, and leaving us to conjecture who the mysterious visitor might be.

II.

"Yes, I allow I'm right glad yer don't mind passin' the night out hyere by the fire," said Josh, taking up the thread of the conversation again upon his return, shortly after. "Wa-all, I was a-tellin' about this queer company of ourn. Came unexpected, same as you did; 'peared all of a sudden out of the woods. It's a leetle girl, sirs; says she's twelve year old, but small of her age - nothin' but a child, though I reckon life's used her hard, pore creetur! Yer should a-seen her when she 'rived. Her shoes war most wore off with walkin', an' her purty leetle feet all blistered an' sore. Mirandy 'marked to me arterward that her gown war a good deal tore with comin' through the brambles, though she'd tried to tidy it up some by pinnin' the rents together with thorns. But, land sakes, I did not take notice of that: my eyes were jest fastened on her peaked face. White as a ghost's, sirs; an' her dull-lookin', big black eyes, that stared at us, yet didn't seem ter see nothin'.

"Wa-all, that's the way the leetle one looked when she stepped out of the shadders. Mirandy was totin' water from the spring yonder, an' when she see her she jest dropped the bucket an' screamed - thought it was a spook, yer know. I war a-pilin' wood on the fire, an' when the girl saw me she shrank back a leetle; but when she ketched sight o' Mirandy she 'peared to muster up courage, tuk a step forward, an' then sank down all in a heap, with a kinder moan, right by the bench thar. She 'peared miserable 'nough, I can tell yer: bein' all of a shiver an' shake, with her teeth chatterin' like a monkey's.

"Mirandy stood off, thinkin' the creetur was wild or half-witted, likely; but I says: 'Bullets an' bombshells, Mirandy' - escuse me, gentlemen, but that's a good, strong-soundin' espression, that relieves my feelin's good as a swear word, - bullets an' bombshells, woman, don't yer see the girl's all broke up with the ague?' - 'Why, sur 'nough!' cried she, a-comin' to her senses. 'I'd oughter known a chill with half an eye; an' sartain this beats all I ever saw,' With that she went over an' tuk the girl in her arms, an' sot her on the bench, sayin', 'You pore honey, you! Whar'd you come from?' At this the leetle one began to cry - tried to speak, then started to cry again. 'Wa-all, never mind a-talkin' about it now,' says Mirandy, settin' to quiet her, an' pettin' an' soothin' her in a way that I wouldn't a-believed of Mirandy if I hadn't a-seen it; for she hasn't had much to tetch the soft spot in her heart sence our leetle Sallie died, which is nigh onto eight year ago. 'Come, Josh,' she called ter me, 'jest you carry this hyere child inter the house an' lay her on the bed. I reckon she can have the leetle room, an' you can sleep in the kitchen ternight.' - 'I'm agreeable,' answers I; so I picked her up (she war as limp an' docile as could be), an' carried her in, an' put her down on the bed. That was three weeks come Sunday, an' thar she's been ever since."

Our host had finished his story, yet how much remained untold! All the care and kindness which the stranger had received at the hands of these good simple people was passed over in silence, as if not worth mentioning.

Josh rose and went to the fire to relight his brier-wood pipe, which had gone out during the recital.

"And is the little girl still very ill?" asked Father Friday, with gentle concern.

"Yes; an' the trouble is, she gets wus an' wus," was the reply. "The complaint's taken a new turn lately. She's been in a ragin' fever an' kind of flighty most of the time. Yer see, she'd had a sight of trouble afore she broke down, an' that's what's drivin' her distracted. She'd lost her folks somewhar way down South, - got separated from them in the hurly-burly of a flight from a captured town; an', childlike, she set about travellin' afoot all over the land to find them. How she got through the lines I can't make out, unless she got round 'em some way, comin' through the woods. Anyway she's here, and likely never to get any farther in her search, pore honey! But what's her name, or who her people are, is more nor I can say; for, cur'ous as it seems, she has plum forgotten these two things.

"Thar's another matter, too, that bothers us some. She keeps a-callin' for somebody, an' beggin' an' prayin' us not to let her die without somethin', in a way that would melt the heart of a rock. It makes me grow hot an' then cold all in a minute, jest a-listenin' to her. To-day she war plum out of her head, an' war goin' to get right up an' go off through the woods after it herself. Mirandy had a terrible time with her; an' it wasn't till she got all wore out from sheer weakness that she quieted down an' fell asleep, jest a leetle before yer 'peared, strangers. What it is she keeps entreatin' an' beseechin' for we never can make out, though I'd cut my hand off to get it for her, she's sech a patient, grateful leetle soul. But" - Josh started up; a sudden hope had dawned upon him as he looked across at Father Friday's strong, kind face - "perhaps you could tell. Bullets an' bombshells, that's a lucky idee! I'll go an' ask Mirandy about it."

That any one was ill or disquieted in mind was a sufficient appeal to the sympathy and zeal of Father Friday. He put his hand to his breast a moment, and I knew that he was praying for the soul so sorely tried.

In a few moments Josh returned, saying, "Mirandy says the leetle girl is jest woke up, an' seems uncommon sensible an' clear-headed. Perhaps if yer war ter ask her now, she could tell yer it all plain."

Father Friday rose, and I followed too, as the man led the way to the little room, the door of which was immediately opened by his wife, who motioned to us to enter. Never shall I forget the sight that greeted my eyes. Upon the bed lay a childish form, with a small, refined face, the pallor of which was intensified by contrast with the large dark eyes, that now had a half startled, expectant, indescribable expression. The sufferer had evidently reached the crisis of a malarial fever; reason had returned unclouded; but from that strange, bright look, I felt that there was no hope of recovery.

How shall I find words to portray what followed! The others

waited beside the door; but Father Friday advanced a few steps, then paused, so as not to frighten her by approaching abruptly. As he stood there in his cassock, with his hand raised in benediction, and wearing, as I knew, the Blessed Sacrament upon his breast, I realized more fully than ever before the grandeur of the priestly mission to humanity. The girl's roving glance was arrested by the impressive figure; but how little were any of us prepared for the effect upon her! The dark eyes lighted up with joyful recognition, her cheek flushed, and with a glad cry she started up, exclaiming, "Thank God, my prayer is granted! God has sent a priest to me before I die!"

Had a miracle been wrought before us we could not have been more astounded. Instinctively I fell upon my knees. Mirandy followed my example; and Josh looked as if he would like to do so too, but was not quite sure how to manage it.

Father Friday drew nearer.

"I knew you would come, Father," she continued, with a happy smile. "This is what I have prayed for ever since I have been lying here. I thought you would come to-day; for since early morning I have been imploring the Blessed Virgin to obtain this favor for me."

She sank back on the pillow exhausted, but after a few minutes revived once more.

It was apparent, however, that there was no time to be lost. I beckoned Josh and his wife out into the kitchen, and left Father Friday to hear her confession. Soon he recalled us. I have but to close my eyes to see it all as if it were yesterday: the altar hastily arranged upon a small deal table; the flickering tallow dips, the only light to do homage to the divine Guest; the angelic expression of the dying girl as she received the Holy Viaticum.

After that we all withdrew, Father Friday and I going out by the fire again. He resumed his breviary, and I remained silently musing upon all that had passed within the last hour. After a few moments he paused, with, his finger and thumb between the leaves of the book, and looked toward me. I hastened to avail of the opportunity to speak my thoughts.

"This, then, is the meaning of our strange wandering in the woods all day, Father," said I. "You were being providentially led from the path and guided to the bedside of this poor girl, that she might not die without the consolations of religion."

"I cannot but believe so," he replied, gravely. "We missionaries witness strange things sometimes. And what wonder? Is not the mercy of God as great, the intercession of Mary as powerful, as ever? To me this incident is but another beautiful example of the efficacy of prayer."

Before long Father Friday was again summoned within, and thus all night he watched and prayed beside the resigned little sufferer, whose life was slipping so fast away. In the grey of the early morning she died.

"Mussy me, I feel like I'd lost one of my own!" sobbed Mirandy.

"Yes, it's cur'ous how fond of her we grew; though she jest lay there so uncomplainin', an' never took much notice of nothin'," said Josh, drawing his brawny arm across his eyes.

An hour later he led the way before Father Friday and myself, and conducted us to the bridle-path, which joined the turn-pike several miles below the town. By noon we were safely at home.

Two days after, however, I again accompanied Father Friday to the forest, when, with blessing, the little wanderer was laid to rest among the pines. One thing he had vainly tried to discover. Though during that night her mind had been otherwise clear and collected, memory had utterly failed upon one point: she could not remember her name. As we knew none to put upon the rude cross which we placed to mark her grave, Father Friday traced on the rough wood, with paint made by Josh from burnt vine twigs, the simple inscription: "A Child of Mary."

HANGING MAY-BASKETS

I.

"I am so glad May-day is coming!" exclaimed Ellen Moore. "What sport we shall have hanging May-baskets!"

"What do you mean?" inquired Frances, who lived in Pennsylvania, but had come to New England to visit her cousins.

"Never heard of May-baskets?" continued Ellen, in astonishment. "Do you not celebrate the 1st of May in Ridgeville?"

"Of course. Sometimes we go picking wild flowers; and at St. Agnes' Academy, where I go to school, they always have a lovely procession in honor of the Blessed Virgin."

"We have one too, in the church," replied Ellen; "but hanging May-baskets is another thing altogether -"

"That is where the fun and frolic come in," interrupted Joe, looking up from the miniature boat which he was whittling out with his jackknife.

"You see," explained Ellen, "the afternoon before we make up a party, and go on a long jaunt up hill and down dale, through the woods and over the meadows, picking all the spring blossoms we can find. Finally, we come home with what we have succeeded in getting, and put them in water to keep fresh for the following day. Then what an excitement there is

MARY CATHERINE CROWLEY

hunting up baskets for them! Tiny ones are best, because with them you can make the flowers go farther. Strawberry baskets - the old-fashioned ones with a handle - are nice, especially if you paint or gild them. Burr baskets are pretty too; and those made of fir cones. Joe has a knack of putting such things together. He made some elegant ones for me last year."

"Are you trying to kill two birds with one stone?" asked her brother, with a laugh. "Your compliment is also a hint that you would like me to do the same now, I suppose?"

"I never kill birds," rejoined Ellen, taking the literal meaning of his words, for the purpose of chaffing him. "Nor do you; for you told me the other day you did not understand how some boys could be so cruel."

"No, but you do not mind their being killed if you want their wings for your hat," continued Joe, in a bantering tone.

"Not at all," said Ellen, triumphantly. "In future I am going to wear only ribbons and artificial flowers on my *chapeau*. I have joined the Society for the Prevention of the Destruction of the Native Birds of America."

"Whew!" ejaculated Joe, with a prolonged whistle. "What a name! I should think that by the time you got to the end of it you'd be so old that you wouldn't care any more for feathers and fixings. I suppose it is a good thing though," he went on, more seriously. "It is just as cruel to kill birds for the sake of fashion as it is for the satisfaction of practising with a sling; only you girls have somebody to do it for you; and you don't think about it, because you can just step into a store and buy the plumes -"

"But what about the May-baskets?" protested Frances, disappointed at the digression.

"Oh, I forgot!" said Ellen. "Bright and early May-morning almost every boy and girl in the village is up and away. The plan is to hang a basket of wild flowers at the door of a friend, ring the bell or rattle the latch, and then scamper off as fast as you can. You have to be very spry so as to be back at home when your own baskets begin to arrive; then you must be quick to run out and, if possible, catch the friend who knocks, and thus find out whom to thank for the flowers."

"How delightful!" cried Frances, charmed at the prospect.

"It is so strange that you did not know about it!" added Ellen.

"Not at all," said Mrs. Moore, who had come out on the veranda where the young folks were chatting, - Frances swinging in the hammock, Ellen ensconced in a rustic chair with her fancy-work, and Joe leaning against a post, and still busy whittling. "Not at all," repeated Ellen's mother. "In America it is but little observed outside of the Eastern States. This is one of the beautiful traditionary customs of Catholic England, which even those austere Puritans, the Pilgrims, could not entirely divest themselves of; though among them it lost its former significance. Perhaps it was the gentle Rose Standish or fair Priscilla, or some other winsome and good maiden of the early colonial days, who transplanted to New England this poetic practice, sweet as the fragrant pink and white blossoms of the trailing arbutus, which is especially used to commemorate it. In Great Britain, though, it may have originated in the observances of the festivals which ushered in the spring. On the introduction of Christianity it was retained, and continued up to within two or three hundred years, - no doubt as a graceful manner of welcoming the Month of Our Lady. That it was considered a means of honoring the Blessed Virgin, as well as of expressing mutual kindness and good-will, we can see; since English historians tell us that up to the sixteenth century it was usual to adorn not only houses and gateways, but also the doors as well as the interior of churches, with boughs and flowers; particularly the entrances to shrines dedicated to the Mother of God."

"And the 1st of May will be the day after to-morrow!"

remarked Frances, coming back to the present.

"Yes. And to-morrow, right after school - that will be about three o'clock, you know, - we shall start on our tramp," said Ellen. "As you do not have to go to school, Frances, you will be able to prepare the baskets during the morning. Come into the house with me now, and I'll show you some which I have put away."

II.

The next afternoon many merry companies of young people explored the country round about Hazelton in quest of May-flowers. That in which we are interested numbered Frances, Ellen, her brother Joe, their little sister Teresa, and their other cousins, Elsie and Will Grey.

"I generally have to join another band," Ellen confided to Frances, as they walked along in advance of the rest; "because Joe does not usually care to go. He is very good about making the baskets for me; but, as he says, he 'don't take much stock in hanging them.' Yet, to-day he seems to be as anxious to get a quantity of the prettiest flowers as any one. Will comes now because Joe does. But Joe has some notion in his head. I wish I could find out what it is!"

Frances speculated upon the subject a few minutes; but, not being able to afford any help toward solving the riddle, she speedily forgot it in the pleasure of rambling through the fields, so newly green that the charm of novelty lingered like dew upon them; and among the lanes, redolent with the perfume of the first cherry blossoms, - for the season was uncommonly advanced.

Before long everybody began to notice how eager Joe was in his search.

"What are you going to do with all your posies?" queried Will, twittingly.

"They must be for Frances," declared Elsie.

"Maybe he is going to give them to Aunt Anna Grey," ventured Teresa.

"Perhaps to mother," hazarded Ellen.

"Yes: some for mother," admitted Joe; "and the others for -

don't you wish you knew!" And Joe's eyes danced roguishly as he darted off to a patch of violets.

"He has some project. What can it be?" soliloquized Ellen, looking after him.

Joe, unconscious of her gaze, was bending over the little blue flowers, and humming an air which the children had learned a few days before.

"That tune is so catchy I can't get it out of my mind," he remarked to Will.

Suddenly Ellen started up. "I know!" she said to herself. Then for a time she was silent, flitting to and fro with a smile upon her lips, her thoughts as busy as her fingers. "Ha, Master Joe! I believe we'll all try that plan!" she exclaimed at length, laughing at the idea of the surprise in store for him. Presently she glanced toward Teresa and Elsie, who were loitering under a tree, talking in a low tone. Ellen laughed again. "Those two children are always having secrets about nothing at all," mused she.

Ellen was a lively girl, and greatly enjoyed a joke. After a while, when she discovered Elsie alone, she whispered something to her. The little girl's brown eyes grew round with interest. She nodded once or twice, murmuring, "Yes, yes!"

"And you must not breathe a word of it to anybody - not even to Teresa!" said Ellen.

"Oh, no!" said Elsie, quite flattered that such a big girl should confide in her.

Then - ah, merry Ellen! - did she not go herself and tell Teresa, charging her also not to reveal it? Later she took occasion to say a word to Frances upon the same topic.

"Splendid!" cried the latter. "I'll not speak of it, I

promise you."

Finally, Ellen suggested the very same thing to Will, who chuckled, looked at Joe, and asked:

"Are you sure you're on the right track?"

"You'll see if I'm not!" replied Ellen.

"Well, all I say is," he went on, condescendingly, "you've hit upon a capital scheme; and you may bet your boots on it that I won't do anything to spoil it."

The girl looked down at her strong but shapely shoes (she was a bit vain of her neat foot), and thought that she would not be so unladylike as to 'bet her boots' on anything. But, as Will's observation was entirely impersonal, and intended as a pledge that he would follow her instructions, she made no comment. Moreover, she had now brought about the state of affairs which she had mischievously designed. Each of the party except Joe supposed that he or she had a secret with Ellen which the others knew nothing about; to each she had whispered her conjecture regarding Joe's purpose, and planned that they, the two of them, should please him by joining in it, without intimating their intention to him or any one. What a general astonishment and amusement there would be when it came out that all had known what each had been enjoying as a secret!

Meantime they had been active, and each had gathered a fair quantity of pretty flowers - arbutus, violets, anemones, and cherry blooms; to which Teresa and Elsie insisted upon adding buttercups and even dandelions. Now the sun was going down, and they gaily turned their steps toward home.

III.

"A happy May-day!" the children called to one another the next morning, as they set out, at a very early hour, upon their pleasant round of floral gift-leaving. Before doing so, however, each had held a special conference with Ellen.

"Yes, I've managed it. Won't everybody be surprised?" she quietly agreed again and again. And yet *how* surprised everybody would be only sportive Ellen knew.

At half-past seven they reassembled for breakfast, which Elsie and Will took with their cousins. What a comparing of notes there was during the meal! Teresa had been caught hanging a basket at her little friend, Mollie Emerson's. Will's mother had seen him dodging round the corner after fastening one on the front gate for her.

"O Joe! what did you do with that beautiful basket you arranged with so much care, - the large one with the freshest flowers, I mean?" asked Frances, with an ingenious air.

"Never mind!" answered Joe laconically, helping himself to another glass of milk.

Everyone stole a knowing look at Ellen, without noticing that everyone else was doing so; but that young lady imperturbably buttered a second muffin, and studiously fixed her eyes on the tablecloth.

"Come, there is the Mass bell ringing!" called Mr. Moore from the hall. A stampede followed. To be late for Mass on May-day would be inexcusable.

Shortly afterward, our friends filed into the Moore's family pew in the village church. As Joe knelt down he turned his gaze with a gentle, happy expression to the Blessed Virgin's shrine. The next moment he started, and cast a glance of pleased inquiry toward Ellen. His sister smiled back at him, then bowed her head to recover her gravity. Hanging from the altar-rail, directly before the statue of Our Lady, was Joe's handsomest May-basket, just as he knew it would be; for he had fastened it there himself the first thing in the morning. But there also were five other pretty baskets, - the offering which each of his sisters and cousins had made, unknown to one another. The pleasant discovery created a momentary flutter in the pew, but that was all - then.

So this was Ellen's surprise! Each silently admitted that it was a good one. When they left the church, however, they had a merry time over it.

"But, Ellen, how did you know what I was going to do with my basket?" asked Joe at last.

"I didn't until I heard you humming the new May hymn which we learned last Sunday," replied Ellen; "that reminded me of what mother said about the old May customs. I wondered if you were thinking of this too, and presently it all flashed upon me."

"Well, if you are not a true Yankee at guessing!" was his only answer.

Choose from Thousands of 1stWorldLibrary Classics By

Adolphus WilliamWard
Aesop
Agatha Christie
Alexander Aaronsohn
Alexander Kielland
Alexandre Dumas
Alfred Gatty
Alfred Ollivant
Alice Duer Miller
Alice Turner Curtis
Alice Dunbar
Ambrose Bierce
Amelia E. Barr
Andrew Lang
Andrew McFarland Davis
Anna Sewell
Annie Besant
Annie Hamilton Donnell
Annie Payson Call
Anton Chekhov
Arnold Bennett
Arthur Conan Doyle
Arthur Ransome
Atticus
B. M. Bower
Basil King
Bayard Taylor
Ben Macomber
Booth Tarkington
Bram Stoker
C. Collodi
C. E. Orr
C. M. Ingleby
Carolyn Wells
Catherine Parr Traill
Charles A. Eastman
Charles Dickens
Charles Dudley Warner
Charles Farrar Browne
Charles Ives
Charles Kingsley
Charles Lathrop Pack
Charles Whibley
Charles Willing Beale
Charlotte M. Braeme
Charlotte M.Yonge
Clair W. Hayes
Clarence Day Jr.
Clarence E. Mulford

Clemence Housman
Confucius
Cornelis DeWitt Wilcox
Cyril Burleigh
D. H. Lawrence
Daniel Defoe
David Garnett
Don Carlos Janes
Donald Keyhole
Dorothy Kilner
Dougan Clark
E. Nesbit
E.P.Roe
E. Phillips Oppenheim
Edgar Allan Poe
Edgar Rice Burroughs
Edith Wharton
Edward J. O'Biren
John Cournos
Edwin L. Arnold
Eleanor Atkins
Elizabeth Cleghorn
Gaskell
Elizabeth Von Arnim
Ellem Key
Emily Dickinson
Erasmus W. Jones
Ernie Howard Pie
Ethel Turner
Ethel Watts Mumford
Eugenie Foa
Eugene Wood
Evelyn Everett-Green
Everard Cotes
F. J. Cross
Federick Austin Ogg
Ferdinand Ossendowski
Francis Bacon
Francis Darwin
Frances Hodgson Burnett
Frank Gee Patchin
Frank Harris
Frank Jewett Mather
Frank L. Packard
Frederick Trevor Hill
Frederick Winslow Taylor
Friedrich Kerst
Friedrich Nietzsche
Fyodor Dostoyevsky

Gabrielle E. Jackson
Garrett P. Serviss
Gaston Leroux
George Ade
Geroge Bernard Shaw
George Ebers
George Eliot
George MacDonald
George Orwell
George Tucker
George W. Cable
George Wharton James
Gertrude Atherton
Grace E. King
Grant Allen
Guillermo A. Sherwell
Gulielma Zollinger
Gustav Flaubert
H. A. Cody
H. B. Irving
H. G. Wells
H. H. Munro
H. Irving Hancock
H. Rider Haggard
H. W. C. Davis
Hamilton Wright Mabie
Hans Christian Andersen
Harold Avery
Harold McGrath
Harriet Beecher Stowe
Harry Houidini
Helent Hunt Jackson
Helen Nicolay
Hendy David Thoreau
Henrik Ibsen
Henry Adams
Henry Ford
Henry Frost
Henry James
Henry Jones Ford
Henry Seton Merriman
Henry Wadsworth
Longfellow
Henry W Longfellow
Herbert A. Giles
Herbert N. Casson
Herman Hesse
Homer
Honore De Balzac

Horace Walpole
Horatio Alger, Jr.
Howard Pyle
Howard R. Garis
Hugh Lofting
Hugh Walpole
Humphry Ward
Ian Maclaren
Israel Abrahams
J.G.Austin
J. Henri Fabre
J. M. Barrie
J. Macdonald Oxley
J. S. Knowles
J. Storer Clouston
Jack London
Jacob Abbott
James Allen
James Lane Allen
James Andrews
James Baldwin
James DeMille
James Joyce
James Oliver Curwood
James Oppenheim
James Otis
Jane Austen
Jens Peter Jacobsen
Jerome K. Jerome
John Burroughs
John F. Kennedy
John Gay
John Glasworthy
John Habberton
John Joy Bell
John Milton
John Philip Sousa
Jonathan Swift
Joseph Carey
Joseph Conrad
Joseph Jacobs
Julian Hawthrone
Julies Vernes
Justin Huntly McCarthy
Kakuzo Okakura
Kenneth Grahame
Kate Langley Bosher
L. A. Abbot
L. T. Meade
L. Frank Baum
Laura Lee Hope

Laurence Housman
Leo Tolstoy
Leonid Andreyev
Lewis Carroll
Lilian Bell
Lloyd Osbourne
Louis Tracy
Louisa May Alcott
Lucy Fitch Perkins
Lucy Maud Montgomery
Lydia Miller Middleton
Lyndon Orr
M. H. Adams
Margaret E. Sangster
Margaret Vandercook
Maria Edgeworth
Maria Thompson Daviess
Mariano Azuela
Marion Polk Angellotti
Mark Overton
Mark Twain
Mary Austin
Mary Cole
Mary Rowlandson
Mary Wollstonecraft
Shelley
Max Beerbohm
Myra Kelly
Nathaniel Hawthrone
O. F. Walton
Oscar Wilde
Owen Johnson
P.G.Wodehouse
Paul and Mable Thorn
Paul G. Tomlinson
Paul Severing
Peter B. Kyne
Plato
R. Derby Holmes
R. L. Stevenson
Rabindranath Tagore
Rahul Alvares
Ralph Waldo Emmerson
Rene Descartes
Rex E. Beach
Richard Harding Davis
Richard Jefferies
Robert Barr
Robert Frost
Robert Gordon Anderson
Robert L. Drake

Robert Lansing
Robert Michael Ballantyne
Robert W. Chambers
Rosa Nouchette Carey
Ross Kay
Rudyard Kipling
Samuel B. Allison
Samuel Hopkins Adams
Sarah Bernhardt
Selma Lagerlof
Sherwood Anderson
Sigmund Freud
Standish O'Grady
Stanley Weyman
Stella Benson
Stephen Crane
Stewart Edward White
Stijn Streuvels
Swami Abhedananda
Swami Parmananda
T. S. Ackland
The Princess Der Ling
Thomas A. Janvier
Thomas A Kempis
Thomas Anderton
Thomas Bailey Aldrich
Thomas Bulfinch
Thomas De Quincey
Thomas H. Huxley
Thomas Hardy
Thomas More
Thornton W. Burgess
U. S. Grant
Valentine Williams
Victor Appleton
Virginia Woolf
Walter Scott
Washington Irving
Wilbur Lawton
Wilkie Collins
Willa Cather
Willard F. Baker
William Makepeace
Thackeray
William W. Walter
Winston Churchill
Yei Theodora Ozaki
Young E. Allison
Zane Grey